JOURNEY
OF THE
IRISH CHILD

Carol Azams

PublishAmerica
Baltimore

First printing

ISBN: 1-4137-8933-1
PUBLISHED BY PUBLISHAMERICA, LLLP
www.publishamerica.com
Baltimore

Printed in the United States of America

Dedication

This book is dedicated to my mum, Bester Epemu, and my dad, Chief Godfrey Abadiofoni, all my brothers and sisters back home, and most especially, to all the suffering children of Africa.

Acknowledgments

My sincere thanks, to my husband, Frank, for his encouraging words of advice to keep the pen on the paper until the end, and also for being my special *Chief Consultant*.

To my wonderful kids, Frank Jnr., Sharon, and Tracy, for their understanding and never complaining about the most commonly used statement in my household, "Mummy is busy," and most especially to my two eldest daughters, Amanda and Anita, for providing the beautiful poems inside this book.

Very special thanks to Aine McDermott, for providing me with the phrase in the Irish language.

Many thanks to Reverend John Stephens and his wife Gillian, Marlene Skuce for their encouraging words of faith, also to all my friends, particularly Gloria Anny-Nzekwue, and Christine Osundu.

And finally, thanks to me for all the hard work.

Contents

Glossary

Agbada – a type of African outfit for men.
Oyinbo – a white person
Sissy-Eko – Lagos girl (Yoruba)
Egusi soup – type of Nigerian soup prepared with melon seeds
Wetin be that? – What is that?
Na wetin be your problem? – What is your problem?
Kobo – Nigerian cent/pence
Naira – Nigerian currency
Ogbono – certain type of seeds used for the preparation of a Nigerian soup
Wahala – trouble
Pikin – Child
Ogogoro – Locally brewed wine
Omo-owoh – Rich child
Nuao, worya? – Welcome, and how are you?
Koboko – Horsewhip
Oga – Master
Akara – Bean cake
Menini? – What?
Keremi – Little
Martar – Girl (Hausa)
Go raib maith agat – Thank you (Irish)
Garda Siochana – Police Force (Irish)
Failte – Welcome (Irish)
Taoiseach – Prime Minister (Irish)

CHAPTER ONE
Call Me Sandy

Hi, my name is Sandra and I'm fourteen years old. I am what most people would like to call a mulatto or a half-cast. This is because my mum is white and my dad is black, and therefore I have a mixture of both black and white genes in my blood. My friends call me Sandy.

Several years ago, my dad had travelled all the way from West Africa to Ireland to study medicine in Dublin City University. While there, he met and fell in love with my mum. Soon after they married, and two years later I was born. After my dad graduated, he got a good job as a surgeon in one of Dublin city's children's hospitals and had not gone back to Africa since then, which means I hadn't been to Africa, nor had my mum.

Although it freaks the hell out of me sometimes that I watch some not-so-good images on television depicting what life might look like in Africa, I still believed very strongly in having a wonderful visit to Africa with my parents someday, if only to meet my grandparents. And whenever that I raised the topic about my worries with Dad, he'd always reassure me that although the general condition of things aren't so pleasant over there with everyone, what I saw on the telly was usually not the case with all the people living in Africa.

On the other hand, Dad told me that the people in his homeland worked so hard to earn their own living and send their children to school. However, my dad is very proud of who he is and where he came from; likewise he instilled the perception in me never to be ashamed to speak publicly about my parental background.

My dad also said that when he was a child, he almost never saw a white person in his hometown. Because his village was located way in the interior, he did not get to see people from the city that often, let alone a white person. But that didn't rule out the possibility entirely. As strange as it might sound, a white person would visit the village once in a blue moon for whatever reason, and on such rare occasions he'd call out to his friends to come and see oyinbo (white person) and they'd all clap their hands and dance around him and sometimes even want to touch his skin just to see how it felt, because the natives thought that all white people were mermaids and therefore lived under the sea. Also, when Dad's family first learnt that he had married *a white girl*, my mum, they bombarded him with all sorts of questions, and grumbled about him marrying someone with a different skin colour. They even told him then that he was making a big mistake, and that his mother had already chosen a bride from the village for him, but my dad refused to listen to any of them. He couldn't care less about what they thought or said about my mum, as to whether she was a mermaid or not. They were entitled to their own opinions as far as he was concerned. He knew that my mum was a human and that he loved her, which was all that mattered to him then, and even now.

Mum and I always looked forward to the day when Dad would take us to Africa and finally introduce us to the family. Dad, on the other hand, had told us many times that such a day would bring a big celebration to the people of his hometown, as many locals would abandon their farms and stay at home to join in celebrating our homecoming.

Personally, I'm a little bit shy when surrounded by so much people, but all the same I really looked forward to that *great* day when I'd get to visit my dad's hometown and finally meet my other grandparents. Guess you know what I mean; I mean my dad's parents.

Nevertheless, Dad came back home from work one day and announced over dinner that we would be going to Africa to spend the Christmas holidays with his family as he was going to be on a work-leave. You can only imagine my joy when my dad first broke the news to us. It would mean much more to me than just a holiday, as my mind was filled with the thoughts of finally meeting everyone in my dad's family.

I knew how much family meant to my dad anyway; Parents, grandparents, uncles, aunts, cousins, nephews, nieces, or even long distance in-laws, it doesn't really matter, the list can go on and on and on and for as far back as possible from one family tree to the other. In fact, everyone is family as far as my dad's culture was concerned.

"I'm so thrilled, Dad, when are we leaving?" I asked in great anticipation.

"Next Sunday," he replied with a broad smile.

"Good idea, darling, I'm excited too," mum said excitedly.

Also, bearing in mind that while the weather is freezing cold over here in Ireland, it is the exact opposite in Africa, as December happened to be one of the hot and dry months, so it's never cold at Christmas.

Even though I was still sitting down in the dining chair, I had already drawn up a picture of all the different things that I'd love to do while there in my imagination, and the list of things that I'd love to take with me. I even thought that I'd love to go to the farm in the village with Dad's mother. In short, I was simply buzzing with so much excitement.

The next morning after eating breakfast, Mum and I

stormed the Ilac Shopping Centre on Moore Street in search of the latest beachwear and the right clothes that anyone would like to take with them on a summer holiday. Thereafter we went into a pharmacy to purchase some other essentials, like mosquito repellent, sun creams, burns gel, antiseptic creams, insect bite tablets, pain killers and tablets for diarrhoea and nausea, you'd think that we were preparing to move into a war zone.

"Its not like we're going to an all-disease environment, so why all the prevention for this and for that, Mum?" I asked.

"You can't be too sure with anything these days, you know, and moreover prevention is surely better than cure. Remember that saying?" Mum told me jokingly, as we both laughed and chatted cheerfully while walking to the car park.

Very early in the morning on the day that we were due to leave Ireland, Mum and I had been so busy packing and re-packing everything just to make sure that we weren't forgetting anything. Dad, on the other hand, had already made arrangements with a cab to fetch us to Dublin Airport so we could catch our first flight to London before boarding another to Africa.

Next thing the phone rang. There was an emergency at the children's hospital where Dad worked. A little girl needed an emergency surgery and there weren't any other qualified surgeons to operate on her, so they wanted my dad to report to work as quickly as possible, and that was exactly what he did without any waste of time. He headed straight to the hospital in the same cab that was suppose to take us to the airport.

What else, Dad had to cancel our much-anticipated trip to Africa all of a sudden. He would do anything in his powers to help save the life of a sick child, and it seemed very obvious to me that his superiors were taking undue advantage of his kind nature at the hospital, after all his leave was supposed to begin that same morning, but they simply didn't see that, or rather wont let him go on leave.

Well, it might sound like I'm the most selfish girl on the

planet, or even a very stupid one for that matter, but I have to admit that I was so, so angry when Dad called from the hospital to tell Mum and I that the journey was going to be cancelled because of a very critical situation at the hospital.

"Why can't they look for another doctor to do the operation on the patient, and have they forgotten that you're supposed to be starting your leave today? We can't cancel now." Mum was talking into the receiver when she picked up the phone, and I knew immediately that we wouldn't be travelling to Africa after all. Because Dad was very obsessed about those little kids, and would not compromise anything to that, he always tried his possible best for them, no matter what.

He spoke very passionately of those sick kids in the hospital wards; he would often refer to them as his little angels, but to be honest I used to feel jealous sometimes when he'd carry on about how sweet and gorgeous some of those kids were. Don't get me wrong; I know that my dad loves me very much but, you know, as an only child, I tend to allow myself play the green eyed monster thinking that my dad preferred his so called little angels to me. Even though I knew very well that it wasn't true that he preferred other kids to me, as Dad would usually say to me anytime that he suspected I was in that odd mood. "Those kids are very sick and they need the greatest love and care in the world. And also, as a children's doctor, I'm feel obliged to give them both the care and love that they deserve. But most importantly, they all have a very special place in my heart, and I always pray that they get healed very quickly so they can go home." He'd take a careful look at me and then add quickly. " And you sweetheart, you have the most special place in my heart, I hope you know that."

I sat down quietly on the floor and began to cry, as I was feeling so sad and very disappointed at the time.

"Dave, I hope you can hear how upset Sandra is about everything and now she is crying her head off. In fact, I don't understand why you should do this to her," Mum said, "and why your work has to come first before our own needs all the time."

"Well, I hope that she doesn't end up in the hospital sick as well from too much crying," said Mum.

"No please, I think that you should stop telling me that— you need to understand the situation at hand, not everyone is good at accepting disappointments about cancelled holidays, especially not one like this," Mum said and continued to talk to Dad over the phone."

"This is so not good Dave, it's not fair on me, and not fair on her, and even your own family in Africa, or don't you ever want me to see them?" Mum hollered into the receiver, sounding very angry, and then she paused suddenly for a moment. I very well understood that Dad was talking back to her as she paused.

"But you could have explained to them that you're taking your family on a special holiday to Africa, and that we were supposed to leave this morning," said Mum all of a sudden.

"Those are the very same reasons that you give every single year. Perhaps there are other reasons why you don't want to take us to Africa to introduce us properly to your family, right?" Mum argued bitterly with Dad, still over the phone.

"Save it, Dave, because I'm sick and tired of hearing the same excuses all the time," yelled Mum.

"Alright, alright. But I'm not sure she'll want to talk to you now anyway, she is very upset right now."

"Sandra, love," Mum called out to me. "Your dad wants to have a word with you."

"I'm not coming, tell Dad I don't want to speak to him," I said snappily.

"Hang on a moment," Mum said into the receiver. She then put down the handset beside the phone itself and came to me to try to persuade me into agreeing to speak with my dad.

"Please, sweetheart," she said. "Try and understand the situation with your dad. You know how he feels about sick kids in the hospital, don't you? It's okay if you feel let down, but I don't blame him in this circumstance. You know we'll find another time pl-ea-se," she said.

"What are you playing at Mum, I thought that you felt angry with Dad too, so why are you now soliciting for him?" I asked suspiciously, tears still dripping down my cheeks.

"Nothing, it's just that I want you to know that your dad needs us to be thoughtful at this moment in time as that little girl is fighting for her life in the hospital," she replied.

He needs to know that we're okay with his decision to stay and carry out the operation, so he can go into the operating theatre in the right frame of mind. Please come and talk to him," Mum said pleadingly as she wiped off the tears from my face with a tissue.

I looked really hard at my mum for a while, wondering if I should or should not speak to Dad.

Once again, my hope to see the place where my dad grew up was quashed, and no thanks to Dad, let him not carry on with his stupid operation, if he like. I thought sadly.

Anyway, as hopeless and pitiful as I was feeling, there was this little thought that lingered in my head telling me that perhaps I should try to see reason and listen to what Mum was telling me.

Well, it is true that Dad didn't set out to disappoint me, it's only because the situation was beyond his control, as usual.

"Thanks, Mum," I said suddenly, and then got up from the floor where I'd been sitting down and crying to go and speak to my dad.

"Hello, Dad, are you still there?" I asked, sobbing.

"I'm right here, sweetheart," Dad said. "How are you feeling?"

"Not fine," I answered.

"Listen, Sandy, I'm so sorry that this problem came up. Don't be too angry with me, I promise to make up for it next time," Dad said, regretfully.

"I'm not angry with anyone, in fact why should I be, I said. I'm just so sad because I thought that I was finally going to meet your family this time, after waiting this long for it. It's never going to happen, is it?"

"Don't talk like that, it will be different next time, I promise," said Dad.

"Why didn't you ask them to find another doctor to operate on the patient?" I said to Dad and began to weep again.

"It breaks my heart hearing you cry like that, love. Look, your mum asked me this same question and to tell you the truth, I'd asked them the question too, myself," he explained.

"And what did they tell you?" I asked.

"They said that I was the only qualified surgeon that they were able to get hold of in this moment," Dad said. "I hope you can forgive me, sweetheart."

"It's okay, Dad. I understand," I said to him sadly.

"Sure, do you really mean that?" Dad asked optimistically.

"Honestly, Dad. But just one more thing, promise me that you'll try your best on that little patient of yours," I said, wiping off the tears, which had been rolling freely from my face, with the back of my left hand.

"Oh, thank you so much, sweetheart. I'll try my best, I promise. I always do. I love you," said Dad, sounding relieved.

"I love you too, Dad, see you later," I replied.

"Hang on a minute, sweetheart, please don't hang up yet. I just remembered something. You know what, you can still take the trip to Africa if you want," Dad said to me on the phone.

"I don't get you, Dad. What do you plan to do about your patient?" I asked, puzzled.

"Your mum can drop you off in the Dublin airport and my brother, Bill, who happens to be in Lagos city at the moment, will meet you at the airport when you arrive over there. What do you think?" he asked, sounding serious.

"What!" I exclaimed. "You don't mean that, Daddy. You

want me to go to Lagos all by myself? This is the most unbelievable thing you've ever said to me, Dad," I said, completely shocked.

"Eh, well, never mind. Just forget I mentioned that," he replied regrettably.

"No, Dad, don't get me wrong, I only meant what a brilliant idea this is. I'm in shock, that's all," I babbled desperately. "Of course I'd love to go to Africa myself, alone."

"Well then, let me speak to your mum about it," Dad said confidently.

"I love you, Daddy," I screamed into the phone receiver before handing it over to Mum, who'd been standing next to me all the time.

"Hello, Dave, I can guess what about you were talking to her."

"And what are you thinking for heaven's sake? Have you gone completely mad or what?"

"Do you really think that I'll sit back and allow you to send Sandra to Africa by herself, somewhere she's never been to before, not knowing anyone out there," Mum retorted angrily.

"No, Dave, no. I simply can't let her," Mum said in a tone of finality. I just stood there like a zombie, not knowing whose side to swing. Dad was giving me a last minute opportunity, and yet Mum too was right. I'd never travelled anywhere on my own before. Then I noticed Mum's voice starting to mellow down.

"Are you very sure about this, Dave?" Mum said worriedly. "Sandra is only fourteen years old, and she is my only child. I don't want her to be exposed to any form of danger whatsoever."

"All right, if you really believe that it is the best thing to do. But make sure that you instruct your brother to look after her very well. I'll see you later, bye," Mum said as she replaced the handset, and then turned to talk to me.

I was quite apprehensive about what Mum was going to say to me about the new development and had thought that I couldn't bear it if she said no, because it would mean a second disappointment in just one day, which would be too much for me to handle. I didn't wait for her to speak first.

"Please, Mum, don't say no. This might be the only chance that I might have to ever travel to Africa. Please say yes," I said, pleading anxiously.

After taking a deep breath, she looked up and stared into the empty ceiling for quite a while. Then she turned to me again, but this time with a little smile on her face. And finally she said yes.

She also asked me to get ready immediate so that she could drop me off at the airport to catch my first flight, which would take me to London where I was going to be transiting for two hours before embarking on a second one to fly me to Lagos.

Mum and I soon got into the car and headed towards Dublin Airport.

She drove very slowly in her usual way at first, but soon as we got on the M50 motorway, she began speeding all of a sudden, as though she had just been possessed by an evil force which was desperate to cause her to lose control of the car. As far as I was concerned, Mum's a very good driver and she'd never ever driven like that before, and I knew very well that something was seriously upsetting her, something which she rather not tell me perhaps. Inside the car there were emotional war going on. Mum refused to switch on the car radio, saying that she was not in the mood to listen to any news, let alone listen to music.

She looked very moody and hardly said any word to me, so I decided to cheer her up, I deliberately brought out the topic about my journey just to find out how she really she felt about it.

"Are you sure you'll be okay without me, Mum?" I asked, concerned.

"Yeah, don't worry about me, I'll be fine, sweetheart. You go out there and enjoy yourself, okay," she said as calmly as she could manage. But that was only a camouflage and she wasn't going to fool me anyway. I took a very good look at her and saw the tears gently rolling down her face.

"You look troubled, Mum—sure you're going to be okay?" I asked insistently. Again she replied that she was just fine, even though it was so obvious for me to see that she was definitely crying.

"I'm not a baby, Mum. And do you seriously believe that I wont see the tears coming out of your eyes, so why don't you tell me exactly what's on your mind about all this," I said to her demandingly.

"Honestly, I'm grand," she lied one more time.

"No, Mum, I know that you're not being completely honest with me, I'm not blind, nor am I a fool. You don't look too pleased with the arrangement, Mum," I said.

After hesitating for while, she then confessed that she was crying really, but that it was not her fault and I shouldn't blame her for crying.

She said that it was probably due to the fact that I'd not been away from home on my own before, and she had not stayed home without me before.

"I'm going to miss you so much, sweetheart, you know that we haven't stayed away from each other before," Mum told me in an emotional tone and both of us cried together.

"I'm going to miss you too, Mum," I said, weeping.

"Hey! Wipe those tears off your face, darling. We shouldn't be crying like babies," Mum said. "This is my fault that you're crying too, isn't it? I know that emotionally, you're stronger and better at controlling yourself."

"Its because the tear's been welling up in my eyes and I've been trying so hard to fight it back, but you know, I'm a weakling when it comes to something like this. I just decided to let it roll. And you know, sometimes when you're feeling very unhappy like it's the end of the world, tears do help."

"I've tried it on more than one occasion and it worked for me. Let the tears roll and you find out you soon feel clear-headed," she explained.

"First of all, let me say that you're not weak, so stop blaming yourself, and second of all, you just might be right about your 'let the tears roll' therapy."

"And it's only natural that one becomes moody and even tearful when their loved one leaves them; it shows how much you love and care about that person. And I love you so much, Mum," I said glumly.

"Hey! You speak so intelligently, Sandy. I was supposed to give you the pep talk instead. I love you so dearly too and I'm so proud of you," Mum said as she tried to hug me with one hand, while keeping the other on the car steering wheel.

"Let me tell you what I've been thinking," she said. "My mind's been whirling with all those stories that your Dad used to tell us about himself when he was growing up."

"Which one of the stories are you referring to, Mum?" I asked hastily.

"Remember the one he mentioned that he and the other children used to dance around and touching the skin of a white person when they saw one?' Mum asked me, and we both started laughing.

"Yes, I remember that story, but that was a long time ago, Mum."

"Wait a minute, Mum, you are not thinking that they're going to swarm around me like bees when I get to Dad's village, are you, and besides I'm not a complete white person, remember?" I said.

"Oh well, but that depends if they're going to see you in that way, your skin is still lighter than theirs, so they might as well see you as a little white girl," Mum replied, teasingly.

When we got to the airport Mum helped me to check in my luggage and soon Dad called to speak to me on Mum's mobile phone to say his goodbyes, but funnily he was almost crying too.

"Sweetheart, I've phoned Uncle Bill to inform him what time you'll be arriving and he is prepared to meet you at the airport in Lagos."

I hope you have his photos with you, and not only that, try to remember that he'll be wearing a brown colour outfit, complete three piece Agbada with a hat to match (type of native African outfit) that will make it easier for you to recognise him, okay?" Dad explained to me before asking to speak to Mum once again. I heard Mum apologising for the little mix-up earlier.

Finally, it was time for me to begin my mystery journey alone as the announcement came through the loud speakers that it was time to board the flight. And it meant also that it was time too for Mum to drive back home, so we hugged each other so tight, as though I was going away forever. Neither of us felt like letting go of the other for a couple of minutes or so, and after that little drama she handed some money to me, with a word of warning though.

"Here is some pocket money for you, please take care and don't lose it okay," she said.

"Thanks, Mum, I'll miss you and Dad so much," I said in a very soft voice. I hardly heard myself.

"And we're going to miss you too, sweetheart. Please, look after yourself," Mum said as steadily as she could manage to control herself.

"I love you so much, Mum," I repeated.

"I love you too, and please call me when your plane lands in London Heathrow Airport, okay," Mum said to me as we hugged one final time.

CHAPTER TWO
Nightmare Flight

"Wow!" I gasped as I walked into the large waiting area of British airways; our flight was delayed for an extra two hours.

Well, it was a great relief after that horrible experience on the flight from Dublin to London.

I watched in awe as some of the passengers panicked when the plane became very unstable in mid-air.

I couldn't see the reason why such a short flight could cause so much terror for everyone on board, and to tell you the truth, I found it was rather funny watching real grown-ups behave in such a helpless and desperate manner.

One man on board prayed like crazy, panting and shouting. Anyway, I can't blame him, he even mentioned that he had a young family at home and didn't want to leave them on their own—three lovely young kids and a beautiful wife, as he puts it.

Like myself and the other passengers also, he must have thought about the worst happening to us—that we were going to crash, as the air instability was so severe causing the plane to wave from side to side, and the passengers to sway in their seats like kids on a swing in a park.

I don't mean to sound so rude, but I was quite amused as I was frightened.

On arriving safely in Heathrow Airport, and I came to realise how something can change within minutes for anyone, thinking that we could have all been dead within seconds if the plane had crashed.

Everything seemed a bit different to me. I'd thought silently to myself that if my mum and dad were there, I would make them take me through the shops in the airport.

Sure there were lots of nice things inside the shops that I would have loved to buy for myself.

I remember the last time that we went on holiday to America as a family. It was a long time ago and I was only nine. I almost got lost in J.F. Kennedy Airport because I'd wandered into the shops without Mum and Dad noticing.

That is just the type of person that I am when it comes to shopping. A real *shopaholic*, especially when it comes to shopping inside airports. But because I'd been terrified with so much fear earlier in the plane from Dublin, I decided not to step anywhere, not even window shopping. Instead, I sat down quietly in the same place until it was time to board the flight to Lagos.

I almost forgot to call Mum to tell her that I'd arrived safely in London Heathrow, despite that horrible situation on the plane. There was no way that I was going to tell her about the nightmare drama during that earlier flight anyway, as I already knew that the next thing she would say was that I cancel the journey immediately and come back to Ireland. I wasn't going to let that happen, because my mind was made up already that I must continue no matter what, even though my heart still trembled with fear about-facing another six hours in the air.

Later, when our flight was called, a long queue was formed really fast and I went on to join the other passengers. Then an airport security guy checked my travel documents and thereafter I went through the departure hall and soon found myself inside of the giant Boeing 707 British Airways plane.

Shortly, a girl neatly dressed in uniform took my boarding ticket from me and after much scrutiny, she said to me, "This is your seat," pointing to an empty seat just next to the window. She was a flight attendant who was soon going to become my tower of strength during the flight, even though I'd acted quite impolite towards her initially.

"Thank you," I said, and went and sat down quietly. Soon after, a lady came and sat next to me, she was a little bit old— you know, like middle-aged—and she was very inquisitive also, as she almost immediately began asking me so many questions.

Unlike in the flight from Dublin to London, I'd had to sit next to a window this time. I was still a bit shaky, though, as a result of what happened during the Dublin-London flight and didn't want to sit next to the window, but changed my mind as I thought that it wouldn't be a matter of where I was seated if anything was going to happen with the plane anyway.

Soon after I'd settled comfortably into my seat a voice came through the loudspeakers, again telling everyone to wear their seat belts, as the plane was ready for take-off.

I tried looking out from the tiny window and a wave of fear swept through me. And then I started to wonder what would happen to me if the pilot suddenly became tired and then fell asleep while piloting the plane, and thereby caused the plane to crash into the mighty ocean.

I'd never had any type of fears about flying before, but my in-flight nightmare between Dublin and London was gradually turning me into a complete freak and I was scared, yet helpless of the situation.

I looked forward suddenly and there she was, the same flight attendant who had directed me to my seat earlier, standing up in front and demonstrating and explaining to the passengers just in the same manner as was in the last flight from Dublin about what we may do if there was a crash.

That was when I became aware of the little monster that was fast moulding up right in my head, and was in the form of a still small voice, which kept telling me that I shouldn't allow the flight attendant to intimidate everyone on the plane.

At first I didn't seem to understand what exactly the voice was trying to say to me. But one thing that I was certain about was that I'd automatically developed a fear for flying, and the feeling was overpowering.

Soon after, there was another voice and this time around, it was asking a question and almost loud too, *"Don't let her do what?*

"Yeah, don't let her do what?" I repeated silently to myself.

However, I tried to interpret in my own way what was going on in my head, but couldn't find any reasonable meanings so I tried to ignore it, but then I soon imagined what it just might be; the flight attendant was trying to build fears inside us (the passengers) and I mustn't allow her.

That was the message obviously, I reasoned, but I didn't have any clue whatsoever about what I was supposed to do in the giving circumstance.

You need to put a stop to this instantly, the voice said again. Only that I had not a single idea what I needed to put a stop to.

I watched as the flight attendant took out an orange colour type of jacket and showed us how to put it on. She raised the jacket up and pointed to a whistle and a tube, which were attached to it, she then showed us how to puff air into it and also how to use the mask. She went on to explain how the mask would help us to breath and told us the tube would help to keep us afloat if we fell into the sea.

She basically repeated everything just like the air hostess in the flight from Dublin to London.

Then I though that if only the flight attendant knew that I was just coming from a difficult flight, she wouldn't carry on and be so elaborate about all this nonsense talk and demonstration about plane crashes.

I was beginning to panic again, and I was getting very angry with the flight attendant and at the same time, I was still hearing all these strange voices in my head. I was also scared that perhaps I was turning completely mad, and it was all for the simple fear of flying, which I didn't have before.

These arguments were going on in my head and it was becoming too distressing to me. *This air hostess is definitely hiding something from all of us; perhaps she knows that something bad is going to happen to this plane, she is sounding very most definitely, she is sounding very positive. And you never know, maybe all of those people who are in charge, I mean the pilot and all his in-flight attendants; there must be a private secret of a definite escape plan to safety for them in case of a crash. And we would be left all on our own to struggle to safety,* Exactly what the still small voice kept telling me, or rather tormenting me with in my head.

All those thoughts and voices had turned my small head into the Dail-Eirean, and it was getting more and more uncontrollable, so I decided to do something about it.

Right there in my head, I'd become the Taoiseach (Prime Minister) and TDs (Members of Parliament) having a question and answer session.

I had to find answers to all the questions in my head. And not so long, I was able to get the answer that I was looking for—a rather bizarre one, though; and that was a decision to challenge the flight attendant.

"Excuse me lady, what the hell are you indicating?" I stood up from my seat to ask the flight attendant.

Immediately everyone started to stare at me as I challenged her, I was being strongly influenced from inside my own head to act that way and didn't care whether I was being looked at or not, but in some way felt like I was making a big fool out of myself. Yet I carried on because my mind had been taken over by the terrifying feeling that we might not make it to Africa safely.

The air hostess only smiled pitifully at me and said nothing to me.

"I think you should sit down and let the rest of us enjoy our flight peacefully," I said to the air hostess.

"Please sit down, darling. I know that you're scared that something bad may possibly happen to us. We're not going to crash, if that's what you're thinking," said the inquisitive old lady sitting next to me. She's only following procedures and besides, it is her job to inform the passengers of what to do in case of…"

"In case of what?" I asked interuptively.

"My dear, no one prays to be involved in an air disaster, not even the flight pilots or attendants so just sit back and enjoy the flight, okay, and nothing bad is going to happen to us," said the old lady once more, who later introduced herself to me as Elena.

"I hope so," I replied and then sat down quietly in my seat.

It seemed to me in that instant that all the confusions in my head had cleared all of a sudden and I was able to relax.

Later, the same flight attendant came to me with a glass of juice and some biscuits on a small tray.

"Hello, how are you feeling now, my name is Tracy. What's yours?" she asked, smiling mischievously.

"And why do you want to know my name anyway?" I asked, guiltily.

"Hey! I'm only extending a hand of friendship here, so don't be too hard on me," she said. "I thought you might be hungry."

"What made you think that I might be hungry, why don't you just leave me alone," I said to the air hostess.

"Sorry, I was only trying to cheer you up, what is that your name again?" she asked inquisitively. I knew that I hadn't told her my name before, which proved to me that she was really making effort to chart with me, and I decided to give in to her teasing.

"I'm Sorry too. Well, my name is Sandra," I said finally.

"Wow! What a coincidence, I have a little girl and her name is Sandra too, although I call her Sandy most of the times," said Tracy the air hostess.

"Really, so you have a little girl called Sandy?" I asked, surprised.

"Yeah, she nodded. She's only two years old and her nana looks after her in my absence.

"My parents sometimes calls me Sandy as well," I told her.

"Nice to meet you, Sandy. I'm really sorry you were so terrified with all the demonstrations earlier. Don't be angry with me please, it wasn't meant to frighten anyone, we only…" Then she began to say again all that Elena had said previously when she was trying to calm me down. It was only a normal routine, blah, blah, etc.

"It's okay, I'm not angry with you now. I was feeling very nervous earlier. And that was because I had a very bad flight coming from Dublin. Anyway, it's nice to meet you too, Tracy. And please forgive me also for being nasty to you earlier on," I said to Tracy, ruefully.

"It's okay to feel anxious during flight sometimes, Tracy said to me, smiling. In fact, almost everyone does feel nervous at some point, but the difference is that some people can handle their nervousness better,"

"Anyway, thanks for the drink and biscuits," I said happily.

"My pleasure, and please do not hesitate to call me if you need anything," Tracy said, patting my shoulders as she turned to go back to her duties.

She's a very kind person after all. I thought silently, nodding my head. By then the plane had already settled in the air and a movie was being shown on the big screen in the front.

Later, I saw Tracy with another colleague pulling a trolley of food and drinks as they served everyone.

The food was nice, I especially enjoyed eaten the jacket potatoes and lamb meat and I must have overeaten because I soon felt like going to the toilet, except that a different type of fear gripped me yet again.

Before ever going on a flight for the first time many years before, I used to have nightmares about falling off from an aeroplane's toilet, and as I suddenly remembered that awful dream, I decided to suppress the feelings of wanting to go to the toilet, and tried to concentrate more on watching the movie on the screen instead. However, I wasn't going to do that successfully for very long as I kept on shifting from sideways to sideways like a pregnant woman about to give birth to a baby.

Elena soon noticed my restlessness, or so I thought as she asked me if I was okay. For a moment I felt like telling her to just leave me alone and mind her own business, but I managed to control myself and not say anything to her so as not to sound rude.

"You see, I told you that everything was going to be fine, I hope you're feeling more relaxed now," Elena said.

I only nodded my head as I was becoming increasingly uncomfortable. I was clearly twitchy and couldn't understand how anyone on earth would mistake that for peacefulness.

It got to a point that I couldn't endure further, you know, the feeling soon became embarrassingly unbearable, and decided to push the call button, which was located under the hand-rest of my seat, if only to save myself from a later embarrassment of messing up my seat in public.

And true to her earlier promise, Tracy didn't waste any time to come to me.

"Is everything all right here?" she asked as soon as she got to my seat.

"Can I talk to you in private?" I asked Tracy as I wrinkled my face.

She looked at me with concern, and then a fleeting look at Elena and back at me once more, and said yes in such a thoughtful manner.

"There are some empty seats at the back if you don't mind," she said.

"Oh, better," I replied as I excused Elena to let me get past her.

As I sat down with Tracy on one of the vacant seats at the back, I told her quite frankly though in a very shy tone that I was very pressed and needed to go to the toilet as soon as possible, but wouldn't because I was too afraid of falling off the plane.

She smiled at me sweetly like a mother would at her naive little child and tried to encourage me to use the in-flight toilet anyway, that nothing of sort would happen. Then she directed me through the aisle to where the toilet was.

When I'd finished and was already back at my seat, Tracy later came to my seat to ask me if it all went well. Also, she had a small shopping bag in her hand; I discovered it was packed full with biscuits, sweets and small packets of peanuts when she handed it to me.

"All these for me, my goodness! You're very kind, Tracy. Thanks very much," I said gratefully and happily.

"It's my pleasure to serve you," she replied simply as she made way for Elena who was desperate to get out from her seat as well, perhaps she'd been pressed too and wanted to go to the toilet.

Tracy then sat down in Elena's seat to have a quick little chat with me.

"I noticed that you're travelling alone, so where're your parents?" she asked fairly serious.

"My parents live in Dublin and that's where I live too, but as you can see, I'm travelling all by myself," I said openly.

"Interesting, so you're Irish. Tell me something, are you on holiday or something?"

"Well, you can call it a holiday if you like. Actually I'm African-Irish, my dad comes from Nigeria and my mum is from Ireland and funny, though, I'm visiting Nigeria for the very first time, and alone," I told Tracy excitedly.

"Wow!" she exclaimed. "You're travelling to a big country

such as Nigeria for the very first time and all by yourself."

"And you know what, I'm over the moon about everything because I'll be meeting my dad's family after waiting for so long for my dad to take me," I said, almost breathlessly.

"Mm, sooth yourself," she replied simply, as her smile seemed withdrawn a bit.

"Yeah, anything wrong in that?" I asked, politely.

"No not really, but I hope that you're well informed about what goes on in Nigeria," she said, sounding a bit startling.

"What are you talking about, if there's anything why don't you tell me what exactly goes on in Nigeria," I said demandingly.

"I didn't mean to alarm you, but didn't your parents say anything to you about Nigeria, anything at all?" she asked, surprised.

"Didn't my parents tell me what," I enquired, panicky.

"Pardon me, but I was just wondering whether your parents are aware that you're on your way to Africa on your own," Tracy said, this time a stern look on her face.

What a dumb question. What does she think I am doing, running away from home, and by the way who said that she can act as my mum now? If it's for all the goody-goody gifts, she better ask to have them back, I thought to myself.

"Sure they're aware that I'm on my way to Africa, how else did you think that I got the money to pay for my ticket? And besides, my mum dropped me off in Dublin Airport this morning," I said.

"Fine then, but would someone be there in Lagos Airport to receive you?" Tracy queried further.

"Yes, my Uncle Bill. He'll be there waiting for me at the airport by the time we land," I replied.

"And you haven't met this your so-called Uncle Bill in person before, I suppose?" she asked.

"Nope, I haven't, but I have his pictures with me. Anyhow, I'm going to meet him in person today," I said, giggling.

"Have you thought of what to do if your uncle doesn't turn up at the airport in Lagos?"

"I haven't really given that a thought, but why wouldn't he be there. My dad already told him about the arrival time, and hopefully he's going to be there in time before we land.

"Good luck then," replied Tracy.

"Apart from that, I can phone my parents to have my flight re-scheduled, so I can go back to Ireland just in case I don't see him. But I know that that won't be necessary. Uncle Bill had promised my dad that he'd wait for me at the airport no matter what," I explained to Tracy.

"Well, Sandy, I don't want you to start thinking wild again. Just continue to be positive that your Uncle Bill will be there at the airport waiting to receive you," she said calmly and stood up to leave, as Elena came back from wherever she'd been.

"That girl is very nice indeed, don't you agree?" Elena asked loudly.

"Yeah, she is, and very generous too," I replied.

I'd had to call Elena my next *seat* neighbour; of course that is precisely what she was on that plane, at least. She couldn't keep her mouth shut for one moment, apart from the times that she left to go to the toilet or perhaps to stretch her legs. She kept on talking to me until it got to the point where I became very bored and irritated and almost told her to shut up for once. But I didn't want the other passengers to think that I was a rude and arrogant person who did not have any respect for the elderly — not that she was old anyway. My parents brought me up to show respect, especially to elderly people.

But additionally, Elena reminded me so much of my other granny (Mum's mother). She sometimes talks as much too, except that I could never get bored with her because she is so special to me, and I ought to show the same level of understanding and patience to Elena as well.

She told me, amongst other stories, about when she and her husband first got married, they'd chosen to go to India to for their honeymoon. And what a long flight it was that she ended up having swollen legs.

However, I stopped listening to her at some point and pretended to have dozed off. And I did actually fall asleep in the end, as I'd only noticed when I felt someone trying to wake me up.

CHAPTER THREE
A Real Melting Pot

"Sandra wake up, wake up, we are about to land," Elena said.

Subsequently, I heard the same voice from the loudspeakers as earlier, when we were about to take off.

"Flight attendants, prepare for landing," it said.

I started feeling very excited at that time, even though I wasn't so sure exactly what lay ahead. I almost wanted to give a thought to what Tracy had said about what I'd do in case Uncle Bill failed to show up, but quickly brushed the thought aside to concentrate on meeting him there in the airport.

And I succeeded in convincing myself that looking forward to seeing Uncle Bill at the airport, and eventually going to meet everyone in my dad's family was all that I should think about, instead of letting negative thoughts to cloud my mind once again.

"Young lady," Elena called. "I reason that your parents had given you sufficient information about where you are going to," she said.

But what is the big deal about where I'm going? First, it was Tracy asking me questions, and now Elena. I wish she would just leave me alone and mind her own cup of tea for once, I thought to myself.

"Where do think I'm going to, by the way?" I asked Elena politely.

"What type of question is this, or where else do you think that this plane is heading to? Of course I know that you're going to Nigeria, I was only wondering what town exactly in Nigeria that you are going to, that's all," she said.

"I'm actually going to my dad's town. Never been there before anyway," I said to her.

"Is your dad's town in Lagos city? Well, don't bother answering that if you don't want to, and never mind me, I'm just a prying old lady," she said softly.

"No, don't say that, I don't mind at all," I said. "My dad is not from Lagos city, and there isn't much he could tell me about Lagos particularly."

"My dad is from Bayelsa State; it's one of the new states that was recently created by the government, I told Elena. My dad told me that Bayelsa State is located in the Niger Delta region of the country."

"You haven't been to Nigeria before, but you seem to know so much about it already, which is amazing because even I didn't know what region Bayelsa State was until now, " she said with a smile.

"Yeah, that's because my dad is Nigerian, and I'm a Bayelsian," I replied cheerfully.

"Um, good for you, so what other thing can you tell me about Nigeria?" she enquired further.

"But you're not Nigerian so why bother, anyway, my dad taught me the little that I know about Nigeria. He also told me that Nigeria is the richest, and most populous country in Africa. Do you think my dad is right about that?" I asked doubtfully.

"I quite agree with your dad, she said. Nigeria is a very rich country, and very big too.

Personally, I've learnt the fact about the populous nature of Nigeria, but I used to mistrust the fact about it being a rich country for the simple reason that in Ireland, most African people had come from Nigeria.

And once when I asked my dad if he knew why this was so, he simply said that it was due mostly to *economic migration*, and when I pressed him to explain more about what that really meant, he replied that it was too much poverty back home that has pushed many of his country people to leave their beloved home country to come and look for better life in Ireland. But many like him had also come either to work or study. Similarly, there are others who had to flee from persecution, you know, people whose lives are under threat in their own countries.

Nonetheless, I still think that these people are very brave, because it is not easy for anyone to simply pack their baggage and leave their country and the people that they love to settle somewhere else.

One thing, though, that I like in what Dad told me about his country was the fact that it is blessed with so many different cultures and traditions: So many people living together in the same country as one but different cultures and different traditions and above all different languages. Dad used to describe it as though Nigeria is a real *melting pot*. Well, I was about to find out the truth for myself.

And one more thing, Dad also told me that because of the many different languages in his country, the people were able to devise a common language as a way for everyone to communicate with each other more easily, especially benefiting the less-educated ones beside the English language. Of course everyone knows that Nigeria was colonised by the British people just like Ireland too, and English remains the official language and is widely spoken, but the other national language is known as the broken English. Elena also knew about the broken English and she later made me to understand how.

"Do you understand the Nigerian broken English?" she asked me later.

"No, that's too difficult," I replied.

"That is true, it sounds very complicated when you listen to it, it takes a proper Nigerian or anyone who has lived there for a considerable time to understand it," she explained.

"My dad said that some other African countries speak the broken English as well, but that the Nigerian type of broken English is most unique," I said, giggling.

"Ah well, it's got splashes of the real English language here and there, but if you're not from that part of the world, you'll be completely lost when you listen to their dialogues."

"Take for example when someone says 'where are you going?' in broken English it sounds like 'where you de go?' or 'what's that?' compared to 'wetin be that?' or 'what's your problem? To 'na wetin be your problem?'" Elena explained as if she taught the language in her spare time.

"Sounds really weird, doesn't it?" I said, astounded.

"You can say that again; however, the people just love it, and some of them like to use it as some kind of secret code in the presence of a foreigner," she explained further.

"My mum gets upset whenever some Nigerian guys come to visit us and they soon begin to speak this broken, or whatever that they call it. Mum used to think that they were gossiping her."

"But wait a minute, Elena! If you're not a Nigerian and you don't live there, then how come you know about all these things," I asked suspiciously.

"No, not exactly, but my daughter lives in Lagos city with her husband and my two grandchildren, they've lived there for over seven years now. And my daughter's husband is Nigerian; they got married in England and soon moved back finally to Nigeria. I always come to visit once every year," Elena explained to me.

"That's incredible, so your grandchildren are just like me—mulatto?" I said smiling.

"You call them mulatto, I call them African-British, and in anyway they're all the same!!!" said Elena teasingly.

"Yeah, whether I call myself a mulatto or Nigerian-Irish, in any case they're the same," I mimicked, as Elena and I began laughing together cheerfully.

"The important thing is, we're all human beings," she said.

"They must really like it there, don't they?" I enquired.

"Yes, they do, most especially the good weather. And not only that, they find living over there very cheap and affordable too," said Elena.

"I thought that you had something very serious to tell me earlier when you asked me all those questions, if I'd been informed appropriately about Nigeria," I said.

"Oh forget that, but you see Lagos is such a big place, any new visitor could easily get lost, and you know, like in every country, you may come across some unscrupulous citizens, so do be careful, okay," she advised.

"Really?" I asked anxiously.

"Hey! I'm only giving a little advice here, certain things do happen every now and then, but there're societal problems everywhere in the world, so you don't let that scare you, okay," she said.

"I'm not scared, else I wouldn't be on this plane alone. Nigeria is where my dad came from and I'm proud of it, and it is very important to know your roots anyway, moreover my dad told me that if you shy away or if you deny your real identity, your identity would deny you one day also. Whatever that means anyway," I said to Elena.

"Your dad must be very proud of you, Sandra, you speak like a very clever girl I must say," Elena said, complimenting.

"I 'm flattered, thanks anyway," I said happily.

Just then the plane began to lower down and I noticed some of the passengers had begun to take photographs with their cameras through the small side windows, and I was tempted to try the same; however, fears that I'd had earlier suddenly enveloped me and stopped me from taking any pictures from up high.

Although Elena tried too, but I don't know for whatever reason, she retreated back in her seat as well after gazing out of the window.

Perhaps she wasn't too sure about it and had to change her mind, or she possibly had some fears too and was only hiding it just like what Tracy told me earlier about some passengers being very good at hiding their fear of flying.

Soon the plane landed on the runway, rolled a bit and then came to a final stop. At that moment I knew that we had landed safely. Both Tracy and Elena had been right, we did arrive safely. It was the Murtala-Mohammed International Airport in Lagos.

Elena turned to me and said smiling, "I told you we were going to arrive safely, didn't I?"

"Yeah, and thanks for boosting my confident about flying and being my friend on the plane," I replied.

Before long, all the passengers started to take down their hand luggage and quickly made their way out of the big plane, and I also took mine and walked alongside Elena and the others like soldiers marching.

At the exit, Tracy was standing there with some of her co-workers greeting and waving goodbye to the passengers.

When I got to where she was standing, she gave me a quick hug and wished me to have a nice stay in Nigeria

It was quite clear that everyone was in a hurry to get out of the airport, as the passengers practically pushed one another in the long slow queue.

Not too long we all walked into the arrival hall of the airport where, we collected our luggage.

A lot of people were outside trying to see through the wide plain wall, checking to see if their expected loved ones had arrived too. I was hoping that Uncle Bill was among them and possibly watching me.

"Welcome to Nigeria," I whispered to myself silently.

Elena and I each took a trolley to load in our luggage and then we walked outside of the arrival lounge, which was quite large.

"What brilliant weather," I thought out loud.

"Very lovely weather isn't it. This is certainly the best part of this country," said Elena.

"This weather is so, so gorgeous," I said repeatedly.

"I come here to be with my grand children, but I must confess that the weather is another major factor," Elena said quite frankly.

I noticed that the sun had gone down, yet I felt very hot. And with the dryness of the weather, the atmosphere looked so brilliant and welcoming too. The Murtala Mohammed International Airport was just as busy as the London Heathrow. Outside, men and women were dressed in colourful native attires. Some ladies wore massive headgears on their heads, while some simply had braids on.

I was pretty shocked to see so many white people in the airport, because there weren't so many of them on our flight.

Uncle Bill was supposed to be holding a placard with my name on it; I glanced around to see if there was any such person.

"Over here, over here," Elena waved to a man dressed in what seemed like over starched uniform.

"That's my daughter's personal chauffeur, he is here to pick me," she said cheerfully.

"Oh really, I said absent-mindedly. Your daughter and her husband must be so rich to have their own private chauffeur."

"Don't be ridiculous my dear," said Elena. "Almost anyone around here can afford to have a private chauffeur."

"Cool, I still haven't seen my uncle anywhere in sight." I said, as my eyes kept going from corner to corner like a searchlight.

"I must go now. I hope your uncle turns up soon, just be patient," Elena said to me, as we hugged and said goodbye to each other.

For a moment, I felt as though my granny was leaving me. And I watched hopelessly as she walked away into a warm embrace with her daughter's chauffeur. I didn't see Uncle Bill anywhere yet, and I felt a sense of loneliness. It must have been because Elena and I had become so close towards the end of the journey, I almost wished I were going with her to her daughter's house.

What will happen to me, should Uncle Bill not turn up? My thoughts had started to run wild again, as I began to look at the faces of nearly every person who walked in my direction just to make sure that he didn't walk past without me noticing. It wasn't the agreed plan, but I had to be sure in case he changed his mind about holding a placard.

I glanced at my watch and thirty minutes later, Uncle Bill had not turned up yet. I began thinking about the possibility of him getting involved in maybe an accident on his way to meet me in the airport. I also thought about other potential causes as well, and all of them were negative thoughts. Those destructive thoughts caused me to become so confused and I started to see all men dressed in similar outfits just like the same, which meant that it was going to be a major problem because I would not be able to differentiate Uncle Bill from the lot if he walked pass me without having a sign with my name.

Virtually all the other passengers that arrived in the flight with me had gone to their various destinations, which eroded my confidence.

"What will I do now?" I queried myself, as I took one quick look around the crowd again to see if I would see anyone like him, yet there was no sign of Uncle Bill still.

I stood there outside the airport with a feeling of dejection. *I am doomed*, I thought just as I looked in front suddenly and

CAROL AZAMS

noticed a tall man dressed in the exact fashion, which Uncle Bill was expected to be, holding a big sign.

I was so happy that he'd turned up in the end. Although I didn't see his front yet, I assumed it had to be Uncle Bill because of his mode of dressing. I was just about to yell out his name when he turned to face me all of a sudden. Sadly, he wasn't my uncle at all. It was someone else, probably waiting for a friend or relative that was arriving from abroad too.

What a disappointment. It made me feel even unhappier. I stood there running through my imagination of what could be keeping Uncle Bill still.

Then there was a policeman walking towards my direction. And I thought that I had to speak to him and explain my situation to him. After all, he was a policeman, he should be able to help me if no one else could. But then I reasoned that if he happens to ask me to follow him to their office, which might be far away from the airport. It will have only one outcome in that case, Uncle Bill might not be a find me eventually when he turns up in the airport.

"Well, if I were you I'd give it a go," I heard a voice telling me, and when I turned around to see who was talking to me, there was nobody. It had only been my imagination at play once more.

However, I thought that it would be wise to listen to it. My dad used to tell me that I should always follow my instincts.

"I better phone Mum and Dad to tell them that I arrived in Nigeria safely." I said to myself, and went back inside the airport lounge.

I approached a man to ask him about where I could make international phone call.

"Right there," replied the man, pointing to a phone booth in a nearby corner before walking away.

Then I reasoned that before anyone could spend money in a foreign country, they must have that country's local

44

currency, so I decided to search for somewhere that I can exchange some euros to the naira.

There was a shop right in front, it looked like a newsagent, and there was also a small board in front of it with the sign of a bureau-de-change.

"Excuse me," I said to the shopkeeper as I walked inside the shop. He was busy arranging newspapers and magazines in the shelves.

He quickly turned to me and said something like, "Menini, keremi-martar?"

I was completely flabbergasted when I heard him speak those words, as I didn't understand what he was saying to me.

"What, don't you speak any English?" I asked, confusedly.

"Hello! Sorry, I thought you spoke Hausa," said the shopkeeper in a happy-go-lucky manner.

"And what makes you think that I spoke Hausa, do you assume everyone to speak or understand your language?" I asked, slightly infuriated.

"Sorry, madam," he said. "I was simply asking what you wanted, little girl?"

"But you do understand English, don't you?" I asked remarkably.

"Yes, you can hear me speaking now. In fact, I speak English very, very well, why you ask?" he queried oddly.

"Never mind, I was only wondering if you understood English at all," I replied.

"You mean, you wonder why I speak English?" asked the shopkeeper strangely.

"By the way, why would you think that I might understand your language, is it compulsory to speak Hausa in Nigeria? And besides, why must you refer to me as 'little girl', you don't even know me. First of all, you called me little girl, and then madam. Do you not know the different between a madam and a little girl?" I asked.

"I'm very sorry, sissy, it's only that I'm very, very fond of my language and I love to speak it as often as possible. But it is not compulsory at all," he explained in his usual manner.

"What again did I just hear you call me?" I asked on hearing another strange sissy-word.

"Hey, my goodness!" he exclaimed loudly. "What kind of wahala (trouble) is this, see—me—see—trouble, this girl."

At that point, I couldn't piece together what he said because he simply switched over to 'broken' English, as he would attempt to speak proper English one second, and the next, he'd be lost in his usual accent.

"What are you telling me this time?" I asked.

"This girl, do you want to buy something from me or not?" he asked accurately.

"If you want me to spend any of my money in your shop then you must, first of all, quit speaking your strange language to me, and also learn to be polite, okay," I said to the shopkeeper.

"Ha-ha," he laughed. "Look at this small girl, I'm sorry sissy, I mean sister. Yes that's exactly what I meant, 'Sister', or tell me if it's also wrong to call you my sister; after all you won't tell me your name," the shopkeeper said, beaming an unwarranted smile at me.

"Whatever, but I'm not your sister anyway, and I don't tell strangers my name," I told him sincerely.

"Okay, if I can't refer to you as sister, what then should I call you?" he asked teasingly.

"And why is it so important for you to call me anything? I asked. I'm only a customer, and I'll be out of here as soon as possible and may never see you ever again, so why bother?"

"Um, let's see, you just might be back here tomorrow, you never know. Anyway, can I call you *young lady* then?"

"Yes, if you must. Will you please now attend to me appropriately?" I asked.

"Yes, please. So what can I possibly do for you, young lady?" he asked humorously.

"You are the funniest person that I've ever seen, I told him. Anyway, I want to exchange some euros to naira so that I can make an important phone call abroad."

"Oho-ooo!" He exclaimed funnily. "I see, so you want to change money. Okay, how much euros, pound-sterling, or dollars do you have?" he asked.

"One hundred euros only," I replied politely.

"This girl, you're rich. So small girl like you want to change one hundred euros, and you call that only?" he asked oddly.

"Will you please stop joking and trade the money for me, I said. I've got to hurry outside."

"Anyway, one hundred euros will give you two thousand five hundred naira," he said, after working the difference on his calculator.

"Two thousand five hundred naira," I repeated.

That much? I wondered aloud surprisingly. Then took the money from him and turned to walk out from the shop, but just then he halted me.

"Hey, sissy, wait," he said. "I mean whatever your name is, I thought I heard you mentioned earlier that you wanted to make an international call, if I'm not wrong."

"And?" I prompted.

"I sell international calling cards here. D-d-do you want to buy one?" he stammered for the first time since I entered in his shop.

"Yes I want to, how much does one cost?" I asked.

"Ah-ah, who told you that the card is costly? One five hundred units costs only five hundred naira," replied the shopkeeper, in his usual peculiar manner.

"And how many minutes can the five-hundred units last?" I asked.

"Hey, this girl," he said. "You are really behaving like a madam—maybe I should call you 'small-madam', after all you've refused to tell me what your beautiful name is."

"Is that another way for you to find out what my name really is? Sorry, but like I said before, I don't tell total strangers my name and I think it's about time that you stop wasting my time," I replied.

"Fine, but to answer your question, I don't have a brother or sister abroad and I haven't made international calls before, so it means that I can't tell you exactly how long the five hundred units on the card would last you on the phone," he said, grinning.

"Thank you," I said to him, as he handed the calling card to me.

I didn't bother to reply to whatever he said to me from then on, as my mind suddenly returned to *worry-kingdom*, which was to find Uncle Bill.

So I hurriedly paid for the five hundred-unit phone card, collected it and left the shop as quickly as possible to locate the nearest phone booth.

Following the instructions at the back of the phone card, I was able to get through to Ireland in no time and the phone soon began to ring, but there was no response, so I decided to drop a short message on the answering machine for my parents.

"Hello, Mum, Dad, I arrived in Lagos safety, but I have not seen Uncle Bill yet. I think I'll have to call you back in an hour or so if he still hasn't turned up by then. Bye for now."

After hanging up the phone, I went straight back outside, dragging my luggage with me.

My heart began to beat very fast, as I thought about the possibility of Uncle Bill not turning up at all.

CHAPTER FOUR
Fáilte

Before I left Ireland, Dad promised that his brother, Bill, would be there at the airport to welcome me by the time we arrived, and we'd then go to the village together. But I wasn't sure anymore. He wasn't there, and I felt so alone in a strange place where I didn't know anyone.

I couldn't understand why, but my uncle was nowhere in sight around the airport, yet all the people who I'd travelled together with in the same flight had all disappeared to their individual destinations and I remained alone. To be honest, it got to a point where I felt let down and so vexed rather than scared. And I'd thought that maybe I should have left with Elena to her daughter's house. At least they'd keep me safe.

I prayed in my mind that nothing bad should happen to Uncle Bill on his way to the airport, because in the event of anything awful happening to him, I'd have no option but to travel back home disappointed as no other person there knew who I was or which village I was supposed to be going to.

I was still in the middle of that confusion when I looked across to the other side of the road and saw a small gathering of people. It appeared that there were some arguments going on, and it wasn't that any of it concerned me, but I couldn't help but be curious. I guess it was due to the feeling of insecurity that I was having in my mind and only wanted something to divert my thinking a bit.

I watched as a certain teenage girl who appeared to be between eighteen and nineteen years old struggled to free her hands from the grips of a young man. Then there was a tall, dark man in the middle of the gathering, and he was yelling at the teenage girl, he yelled so loud it wasn't a problem for me to hear him from across the road.

And the argument seemed very tensed. I began to wonder what could have caused the arguments in the first place. I thought that perhaps the young lady had stolen something from someone and he was trying to get her to the police, or the girl might have suddenly bumped into a former debtor.

One woman soon crossed the road from the other side and she started walking towards my direction, she had small baby tied on her back. Then another passer-by stopped to enquire from her what was going on across the road. As they spoke in simple and correct English, I was able to understand her explanations about what was going on over there. I heard the woman explaining to the passer-by that a certain village man smacked a young girl with his walking stick for simply walking past him without first greeting him. The village man became annoyed because he felt that young people living in Lagos city were arrogant and had no respect for their elders.

In his opinion, young people, especially teenagers ought to show respect to the elderly by at least greeting them whenever they met them anywhere.

I could not help to laugh when the woman said that, it would have been nice and sweet if young people actually did that, but it sounded funny to me. I thought that to really smack or beat up a total stranger in the streets for not greeting every single old person they came in contact with was really going overboard. However, the teenage girl, like what I'd probably do, did not take the matter calmly with the village guy, so she'd grabbed his flowing robe and tried to beat him back. What I'd been watching were the on-lookers trying to separate the unnecessary brawl between the girl and the village guy.

Later I saw the same 'village man' who'd been in the middle of the scuffle crossing the road. I'd also suddenly become aware that a little girl was in his company, not a very little girl, but she looked about my age. And as he crossed the road with the girl by his side, I noticed a look of familiarity and I'd wondered if I had seen him somewhere before.

But that could not have been possible for the fact that I was only coming from Europe, though I did not completely rule out the possibility that I might have seen him somewhere in Dublin.

"No way, this is impossible," I thought out loud when suddenly he brought out a small placard and raised it up in the air, my name was written on it.

The same man in that embarrassing argument was Uncle Bill, no wonder he looked very familiar. He had a striking resemblance to my dad, especially his nose and eyes. I immediately reached into my backpack and pulled out Uncle Bill's photo, the only one that I'd brought with me. It was he all right.

Uncle Bill stopped in his tracks the moment he caught sight of me as he crossed the road. Then he looked at me properly, looking both ways as I waved at him, just to be perfectly sure that I was the person he had come to meet.

"You must be Sandra, is that correct?" he asked in the manners that a head-teacher would a pupil inside his office.

"Yes, I am," I replied. "And you must be Uncle Bill."

"Wonderful!" he exclaimed with a broad smile.

"I've been waiting for quite a long time for you, Uncle Bill," I said to him.

"He-he-he," he laughed instead. He seemed to ignore my question. "This is my beautiful niece, who has come all the way from Europe all by herself," he said so loudly that it would be better if he used a microphone to announce to the entire crowd in the airport, because at that point people had started to watch us.

"Nice to meet you, Uncle Bill," I said to him, gesturing a handshake in a bid to stop him from an outrageously loud welcoming speech. But Uncle Bill ignored my stretched out hands and grabbed me to himself for a big hug instead.

"Welcome my daughter," he said to me. Although you're a girl, you look just like my brother."

"Thanks, Uncle Bill," I said.

"You know what, among all my brothers and sisters, your father was the only one who looked exactly like my mother, and now you are just like a miniature of her," Uncle Bill said.

"Thanks, Uncle Bill," I repeated respectfully, even though I knew he was over-exaggerating, but because of his behaviour earlier with the young girl across the road, I knew that it was only a matter of time before we clashed.

It's not that I'm disrespectful, but I don't see myself stopping to greet every single person that I encounter on the way just to please him.

But Uncle Bill was quite right though, because my dad told me the same often times that I reminded him of his mother.

I was feeling very tired now from the long flight and the lengthy wait, to make any meaningful conversation but Uncle Bill carried on talking, asking me questions about my flight and my parents, especially my mum, whom he had yet to meet.

"I have waited all these years to see you and your mother, so why did she not come with you?" he asked.

It was obvious that Dad must have explained to him on the phone that I was visiting alone, but because of his persistent enquiries, I managed to give some reasons to him why I had to take the trip alone.

"This is your father's land and you're very welcomed," he said one final time before suddenly remembering to introduce the young girl who he'd come to the airport with.

"I'm sorry, I almost forgot to introduce your cousin to you. Please meet my daughter, Becky," He said, exchanging glances between the young girl and me.

I'd guessed right before, Becky looked just about the same age as me, but only a little shorter. She had come with Uncle Bill to the airport to welcome me.

"Hello, Becky, nice to meet you," I said.

"Hello, nice to meet you too," she replied rather shyly, as we shook hands.

The three of us walked together to the taxi ranch across the road shortly as Uncle Bill lifted my big baggage on top of his head. The sun had gone down totally, but I was still feeling sweaty, and at that point, I could imagine myself taking a cold shower and a lying down in an air-conditioned room afterward. Uncle Bill signalled to one of the taxi-drivers to take us.

"Where are you going to?" the taxi-driver asked Uncle Bill.

"Apapa," Uncle Bill replied, shouting to the driver as if he was deaf and dumb.

"The fare to Apapa costs two thousand, five hundred naira," the driver told Uncle Bill.

"Two thousand five hundred naira," Uncle Bill repeated. But that is way too much; I don't have that much money."

"How much then can you afford?" the taxi-driver enquired.

"Eh, I, eh, let me see. I c-can pay you one thousand naira," Uncle Bill stammered, dipping his right hand into his trouser pocket, probably to check if he had the complete fare.

"You 're definitely going to pass the night in this airport, no taxi here will take you to Apapa for such a small amount," the driver said, presumably.

"All right in that case," said Uncle Bill. "I'll add five hundred more to make it one thousand, five hundred naira. What do you think?" said Uncle Bill.

"Okay, but you should know that it's because of these two beautiful daughters of yours, I'll accept the one thousand five hundred naira, come on—let's go," said the taxi-driver readily.

"Anything you say, can you now please open the booth so that I can load in the baggage," Uncle Bill said to the driver.

Soon we were inside of the taxicab, Uncle Bill sat in the front passenger seat and Becky and I relaxed in the back seat, except that I wasn't that relaxed because I'd been feeling uncomfortably hot, not withstanding the fact that the driver had turned on the car air conditioner, and it was beginning to cool.

Then I tried to wear my seat belt, but I noticed that there weren't any in the back seat and I wondered why any sane taxi-driver could be on the road without having a single seat belt fitted in his car. In Ireland my parents wouldn't dare move our car out in the road without wearing their seat belts, and they always ensured I wore mine as well. I became worried for not wearing one, at least with the speed he was driving at, but Uncle Bill and Becky didn't seemed bothered about it at all.

I was very tired, but still tried to challenge the driver after noticing that he wasn't wearing one either.

"Excuse me, driver, why are there no seatbelts in this car?" I asked calmly, but firmly like an investigative journalist.

"Mm, my dear, don't worry about seatbelt, it doesn't matter if there's none," the taxi-driver said, callously.

"Tell me why I shouldn't be worried not wearing a seatbelt," I questioned.

"Let me tell you, I've been driving for so many years, and there hasn't been a single seatbelt working in my taxi," he said and seemed to brag about it, which really annoyed me.

Clearly he didn't care about the lives of those that he carried in his taxi, or even his own life. And I couldn't understand why such a person was allowed driving on the road in the first place.

"And what about the police, aren't you afraid of them?" I asked.

"What about them, does the police own my car?" he replied heedlessly.

"You mean as a cab driver, you don't know that you could get yourself into serious trouble if you're caught driving without wearing a seatbelt?" I queried.

"How do you mean?" he asked.

"As the driver of the car, it is your responsibility to make sure that seat belts are securely fitted in you car for the safety of your passengers," I pointed out as though I was an officially appointed law enforcement agent.

The taxi-driver started to laugh hysterically as if without a care in the world. And I wondered what I'd said that amused him that much. Then all of a sudden he started to speak again.

"Hey, who told you that the police will stop me simply for not wearing a seatbelt," he said and started to laugh again.

"What's so funny? I asked.

"Ha, ha ha, this girl you're very funny. Very, very funny," he said, turning to look at me in the back seat.

"No, I'm not being funny at all, I think that you're the funny one here. This is a serious matter, and you don't even care about what happens to other people?" I retorted.

He turned to me briefly once again and urged me to calm down.

"Please calm down, sissy," he said.

Here we go again, he calls me sissy also, just like the shopkeeper inside the newsagent in the airport. Um, I'm sure that every young girl around here are simply referred to as sissy.

However, I tried to explain the significance of a seatbelt in the car to the driver and surprisingly, like Elena, the old lady on the flight, he'd told to me respectfully that I was an intelligent girl.

"Oh yes, driver! She is an intelligent girl; we all are in my family. It runs in our blood, you see," Uncle Bill said unexpectedly, bragging to the taxi-driver.

"Oga," (master) he called to Uncle Bill and told him that judging from how I spoke, it appeared that we were coming from abroad. Uncle Bill asked if that wasn't too obvious, as he'd carried us from the international airport to begin with.

"Yes but not all of us, though. This is my daughter only. She lives in Europe with her parents, you see, and her father is my younger brother. He is a top surgeon in a children's hospital you know," Uncle Bill told the taxi-driver proudly.

"But then how come she is white?" asked the driver.

"She is not completely white, can't you see that she is mixed?" replied Uncle Bill.

"So sissy, what country in Europe do you come from?" the taxi-driver turned to ask me, as he tried to concentrate on his driving at the same time.

"I come from Ireland," I replied sharply.

"Which Island do you mean?" he asked, sounding fairly confused.

"No, I didn't mean that sort of island, I mean the one which Dublin is the capital city.

"Oh, yes, I remember now," he said. "Ireland?" (As in, *Iray-land*)

"Yeah, that one I suppose," I responded politely.

"Mm, I see, do you know that one of my mother's cousins lives in your country—her name is Mary, do you know her?" he asked optimistically.

"I'm sorry I don't, because there are so many black people from all over Africa, as well as other parts of the world living in Ireland, so it isn't possible for me to know your mother's cousin Mary particularly."

"Moreover, everyone in Ireland doesn't just know every other person," I told the taxi-driver bluntly.

Surprisingly, he looked at me like I wasn't telling him the truth.

Well, mother's cousin or was it cousin's mother? Either

way, that question was quite confusing, and kind of complicated too.

"So does the police in your country arrest drivers for not wearing seat belts?" he asked later as he started to pull out into the expressway.

"Certainly," I answered. "If you're driving without your seat belts on and you get caught by the Gardi, you could have up to six penalty points at once, which will eventually lead to a ban from driving for up to twelve months or as the case may be."

"Are you talking about the police or security guards?" he asked.

"I meant the Garda Siochana, that is what we call the Police Force in Irish, I said. This is because Ireland has its own language besides English."

"Oh my God!" Exclaimed Uncle Bill suddenly. I never knew that Ireland had a different language, despite the long period my brother has lived there."

The taxi-driver turned to me again, asking whether I was visiting alone, as though he had only noticed all of a sudden. He barely missed hitting the car in front of us by braking abruptly, when I answered positively that I was visiting alone, because in his opinion, he thought that was way too much freedom for a child my age to be travelling all alone. He went further to ask me to teach him a little bit of Irish, for example how the Irish people greeted, "welcome."

"Failte, it means welcome," I said.

"Okay then, Failte, I say to you," said the taxi-driver amusingly.

"Go raibh maith agat," I replied.

"Excuse me, what did you mean?' he asked, bewildered.

"I thought you wanted me to teach you a littel Irish, I said 'go raibh maith agat' it means 'thank you.' You said welcome to me, and I replied to you, saying thank you," I explained, as we all laughed.

"I am totally confused here, I'm not sure that I can speak Irish even if I lived a hundred years in Ireland, I would never be able to speak that type of language, it sounds so complicated," the taxi-driver said, quite honestly.

The traffic was beginning to slow down. I stared out of the car window and watched as men; women and children were hawking all different kinds of wares; from bottled water, canned and packet juices, ice creams, to newspapers, biscuits and other things, all beckoning on vehicles passengers to buy from them.

Then I saw a girl of just about eight years old, carrying a bucket full of cold soft drinks on her head.

"Buy your cold drinks," she said, sporadically.

I was a little bit shocked seeing such a young child with a big bucket carefully balanced on her head and hawking in between vehicles. I know that if any child as young as that was seen anywhere in the streets of Dublin or Ireland as a whole, hawking any wares or products openly in the manners that I saw them doing in Lagos city, the parents of that child or children would definitely land themselves in deep trouble with the *Garda*, and may even end up having their children taken away from them by welfare officers, because such a thing is known as child labour, and it is also against the law and humanity.

And it is so much pity that those poor kids have to struggle that hard in order to support their family, even as young as they are.

I soon felt like drinking something, and asked Uncle Bill if I could buy some cold drinks from the little girl.

"I'm feeling very thirsty, Uncle Bill," I said. "Can I buy some from that little girl?"

"Sure, you can," said Uncle Bill as he began winding down the front car window to call out to the girl.

"Hey sissy-Eko," Uncle Bill called to the girl. "I want to buy some of your drinks,"

"Excuse me, sir, how many cans do you want?" the girl

asked as she came nearer to the taxi, smiling sheepishly.

I noticed she had a slim gap between the two front teeth in her mouth as she smiled. She also looked emaciated as if she'd been underfed since the day that she born, but beneath that malnourished frame, you could see the strength and the determination to keep going in her. I was the one that was feeling sorry for her; she had no idea about any other kind of way that she was suppose to live her life as a young child. And for her and her friends in the streets, it was simply a matter of ' you don't miss what you don't have'.

"You can see that we're four inside this car, so bring us four cans of drink," Uncle Bill said to the girl.

When it was time for Uncle Bill to pay this little girl, he couldn't find the money to give to her. He said that the girl might run away and not return any change if he paid her with a higher note, and therefore asked her to look for the change before he can give her the money for the drinks.

"You know them, these kids, they're all cowboys even though you're seeing them so small, they'd disappeared without returning my change many times before," said the taxi-driver, urging Uncle Bill not to part with the paper note of five hundred naira, which initially, he'd wanted use to pay for the cold drinks.

"But we have to pay her for the drinks, Uncle Bill," I said, almost yelling at the driver and Uncle Bill.

"Sure, we would, but first let her go and look for the change from her colleagues before I hand this note to her," said Uncle Bill.

But personally, I thought that Uncle Bill was wrong just in case the traffic eased suddenly and we had to drive away when she was gone to look for the change for him.

I didn't have the stomach for it, and I devised a simple plan to let the poor girl have her money.

"I think I have the exact amount; I changed some euros in the airport earlier," I said as I deepened my fingers into my purse to fish out some money. But instead of the exact amount in local currency, I handed a ten-euro note to the little girl.

She basically grabbed the money from my hand and started to dance, waving it in the air and singing, "I got dollars, I got dollars."

I wonder if she knew the difference between dollars, pound-sterling or the euros. Clearly, the value of her drinks wasn't any closer to ten euros, but I'd given that much to the little girl only because I felt sorry for her. Although my good gestures didn't go very well with Uncle Bill, he grumbled about why I wasted my money in such a reckless manner.

Becky had been very quiet all the time, and I thought that perhaps she didn't speak English or maybe she was plain shy; after all, many people can become shy when they meet people newly or if they're with strangers. My dad once told me that he used to feel so shy when he was in secondary school that he actually refused to take up the position of school prefect, because he'd be required occasionally to address the students publicly and in English. And he couldn't do that openly, as the only times that he spoke English in school were when he was either reading out from a school text book or novel, or simply answering questions to his class teachers. Other than that he and most of the students communicated only in local dialect, not minding the school rule, which said, "No speaking of vernacular." However, all that came to a stop one day when he found himself speaking English to a new student who didn't come from the same tribe as him, and as he turn around to leave, he noticed that his best friend had been standing there watching and listening to him all along. As funny as it may sound, my dad said that he wished for the grounds to open and swallow him up that day, because he was so embarrassed. It was for him as though he was caught stealing.

One good thing came out of the incident, though; from that day going he was never ever shy to speak English publicly, even though he already missed his chance of becoming school prefect.

CHAPTER FIVE
Survival of the Fittest

After we'd been going for a while, I turned to Becky and asked if she was okay.

"I'm fine," she said sharply, which to me suggested that she was a smart girl after all.

"All those kids hawking about in the streets, do they go to school at all, and why do their parents allow them out to hawk about in such manners?" I asked Becky openly, and also in the hope to stir up a conversation with her.

"I don't know," Becky answered casually in a very soft tone.

"Do you know that in my country, people don't hawk in this fashion, and little kids especially are supposed to be indoors watching television and or playing with the latest video games when they're not in school."

Most especially a little girl like the one we bought the drinks from would be out shopping with her mammy," I said in a jovial way, but Becky only looked at me casually and said nothing. She stared into the roof of the car as if in a trance.

I wasn't so sure then whether she was interested in the conversation at all, she just seemed so moody and withdrawn. I carried on regardless.

"Do you know that every child in my country is entitled to a monthly allowance? It's known as 'child benefit' I reckon you haven't heard of it before, have you?"

And as I said that, she looked at me very, very strangely, yet I couldn't work out why. Did she not like me, or was she expecting to see a totally different person? I thought that perhaps she was expecting to see a complete black girl like herself so we could have more things in common. And I couldn't tell if she felt disappointed that I was mixed colour, but she couldn't possibly have thought that, because she must have known right from time that my mum was white, and I was bound to have mixed colour skin. You know, that makes me who I am now, a proper mulatto, or rather, a white girl in black skin, or is it a black girl in white skin. Think about it very well and you'll not see much difference in that. Ha, ha.

Becky was the first I'd seen of many more cousins who I was going to meet, and likewise she looked my age and I thought that we could bond very well, at least during my stay with them and I wasn't prepared to give up or allow the stupid skin colour thing to put any barriers between the two of us.

So I kept trying, determined to bring her out from her frozen conclave or extreme shyness that has shrouded her entire being or whatever it was, so that I would perhaps have that cousin-to-cousin type of friendship with her. I mean the type of friendship whereby you're almost like sisters.

"Like I said earlier, in my country every child gets his or her own benefit money from our government, that is why no child goes out to hawk in the streets.

"And ideally, no child is suppose to struggle like this anyway; It is not fair on them for goodness sake, they're only kids," I moaned and noticed that my mind had started to go tip top—tip top as I immediately remembered all the horrible stories which I'd read from a history book about *child labour* long time ago. How unfair it was for the children at that time.

Thankfully, that was a very long time ago and I wasn't born yet, nor were my parents.

My mind wouldn't stop wondering about the one question, why child labour was still been practiced in this civilised age. I did not realise that I had wondered out loud about the question until the driver spoke to me.

"Young lady, pardon me, but I've been listening to your conversation at the back there and I have this to tell you," said the taxi-driver.

"You should count your lucky stars, my dear, you are talking about the new age in the western world where everything is perfect. This is Africa where it is a matter of 'survival of the fittest', everyone has to struggle for his or her own survival, whether small children or not.

"Nothing is free here, you see. Unless you struggle like those little children you see out there, you won't have anything. Not a chance of anything, as you're seeing those kids struggling to sell whatever they're carrying inside those big buckets and cartons on their heads, some of them their whole family depends on whatever gain that they make to survive, no matter how little."

"Things are so hard nowadays, you know, and that is why those who have relatives overseas often ask them to send money home," the driver explained.

"That reminds me, Uncle Bill, Dad said something about sending some money to you by wire transfer," I said to Uncle Bill.

"Oh yes!" Exclaimed Uncle Bill. "I already knew that, he told me on the phone when he called this morning to inform me that you were coming," Uncle Bill said happily.

"Lucky you, you have a brother who sends you money regularly from abroad," the taxi driver told Uncle Bill.

"Know what? There's an important story, which I'd like to tell you later," Becky whispered into my ear.

"Really, whatever it is, I can't wait to hear it," I told her also in a small whispery voice.

"I don't mean right now in this car. Later, okay," she said. "Okay," I replied with a smile, hoping that Becky was finally coming out of her shell.

The traffic in the road got so bad later, vehicles moved at a snail's pace. I was still so hot and I asked the driver if he could wind down the car window to let in some fresh air, but he replied that he'd better not try to or else the dust outside would soon fill the car, and moreover I was better off with the air conditioner.

Shortly, Becky started to complain that she was feeling hungry, so Uncle Bill bought some biscuits and more drinks from other kid traders along the way. They seemed to line everywhere in the streets and wherever there was slow traffic in the motorway with their wares.

From all indications in the short time that I'd spent in the traffic, I could tell that Lagos city was a hectic place. There was so much noise everywhere and cars, buses and big lorries and trailers blaring their horns. Although the windows were all wound up I still felt like my ears would go deaf any second.

There was a big yellow bus that was parked by the roadside; it looked just like some of those American school buses that I'd seen before in the movies. There had been so much struggling, people yelling and pushing at each other; a woman practically threw her young child into the bus. At first I thought that they were fighting with each other and I'd been terrified that someone would throw a piece of stone and smash the window of the taxi and hit us. I asked the taxi driver if he had any idea why those people were fighting on such a busy road, and no one cared to call the police. I was flabbergasted by his reply. Instead of him answering my question directly, he turned to Uncle Bill and said something like, "I can see that your niece has a lot to learn about this place, and I hope you educate her about how the system works here," and he then turned to speak to me as well.

"My dear, that spot is a bus stop and they're only struggling to get on the bus so they can get home before it becomes too dark, they're not fighting."

"And you see that big bus, it's the Lagos city bus service," he said, pointing to the big coach on the roadside.

"You mean they have to struggle that much just to get on the bus, why can't they just queue in a line and then take turns to go inside quietly?" I asked openly.

"Many people consider forming a queue as time wasting, so they just struggle for a space in the bus, if you're strong enough then good luck, but if not, sorry," Becky said.

"You're joking, what if there are little children who are hurrying to get to school on time, does anyone help them to get in fast?" I asked naively.

"You still don't get it, Sandra, it is simply how the system works here, children or not, they have to try their best to get in like everyone else," explained Becky.

There was one lady in particular that I felt sorry for, she had a tiny baby tied to her back and was struggling with all those people. I hadn't seen anything like it before, and I wondered what it would be like in the marketplace, if there were so much confusion only for passengers to get on the bus in a common place such as a bus stop.

Well, I quickly brought out my camera and took a quick snapshot of those people hustling each other just for a space in the bus so to I could show my friends back home so they'll believe me if I told them what I'd seen at the bus stop.

Later the taxi driver diverted into a tiny road just off the motorway, the road was not paved and full of potholes. There were small shops on both sides of the road, hair dressing salons, restaurants, a pharmacy and a multi-story building, one of which was the hotel that we were going to stay in.

There wasn't any more traffic, but it was getting really, really dark and I was glad that after spending all the time in the traffic, we had finally reached our hotel.

"The first thing I'm going to do is take a shower, then eat whatever food that I set my eyes on, and then lie down and watch telly," I said to Becky.

"Me too," she replied.

There was no cause for me to think about food poisoning, because I'd sampled different types of African dishes with my dad and my tummy was just fine with all of them.

Soon the driver stopped the car right in the front of the hotel.

"Failte!" the taxi driver said to me, as he stretched out his hand to receive his fares from Uncle Bill.

"Well done, you still remembered," I told him politely and turned to the direction of the entrance of the hotel.

Uncle Bill pulled my baggage, and the three of us walked into the reception hall of the beautiful Day-Spring Hotel, as the automatic door slid welcomingly open.

Inside the large reception hall of the hotel, there was a small shop, which had several items in display, such as wood carvings, toiletries and handmade beads amongst other types of jewelry.

Then I looked straight in a corner and saw an old, frail-looking man sitting quietly in a chair on his own. He seemed not to be minding anything else or anyone else for that matter, but his pipe. It must have been the long pipe in his mouth that had me drawn to him, as I could not help wondering why someone that old still smoked pipes in the first place.

Uncle Bill went upstairs with the receptionist, probably to find out the conditions in the rooms.

As Becky and I sat down alone in the reception area and waited for their return, being the probing type of person, I thought perhaps that I should get closer to the old man and have a little chat with him.

When I walked closer to the old man, I noticed that he looked really weak and tired. I couldn't help my curiosity to touch him; but he did not respond or move his body and I thought most likely that he'd fallen asleep. Though his lifeless body triggered some fears inside me and I raised an alarm, thinking that the old man must have suffered heart failure or something.

"Would someone please call an ambulance, this old man here doesn't look too well," I screamed so loud that everyone present looked to my direction.

"Where is the he, the old man that you're talking about?" asked a young guy in security uniform.

"Look at him here," I replied, pointing down at the old man who still maintained a lifeless posture.

"Just leave it alone, it's fine," said the security guy, as he smiled.

"How can you be so callous? I can't even believe that you're referring to the old man as 'it' as though he was a piece of furniture," I said furiously.

"That's exactly what it is. A piece of furniture of course," the security guy replied like he really meant it.

"What?" I asked, worriedly.

"You heard me correctly; there's no need to panic, it isn't a person," he said, reeling like a laughing jackass. I marvelled at the extent of his joke, and thought that possibly he didn't have any of his grandparents still living, else he would not behave so unsympathetically towards the old man.

"Please just go and call the ambulance and stop these stupid jokes, his life's in danger," I said in a panicky voice.

"Please calm down, said the security guy once again.

When he was convinced that I'd calm down enough to listen to him, he then explained to me carefully that my so-called old man was actually a piece of wood carvings only, and even though he'd been dressed cleverly in a pretty human outfit, he wasn't real at all. However, I still looked back at him with gratuitous pity as I walked away from *it*.

I felt so stupid and embarrassed afterwards. I guess the taxi driver was right, after all. I still had so much to learn about the place. But I admit that the person that did such an excellent job out of ordinary woods must be exceptionally gifted with his craft.

Later Uncle Bill came back with the keys and the potter helped us upstairs with our luggage. Everything in our room was pink and purple, it looked so like a girlie's bedroom. The double bed was neatly covered with a pink, flowered cotton cloth with matching pillowcases and window blinds.

There was a small colour television, which showed a lot of foreign channels, and there was also a fridge and an air-conditioning system in the room buzzing out cool air. I jumped about excitedly like a small baby.

In the smaller room, there was a single bed, as well, covered with the same pinkie and purple stuff. Although there wasn't a television set or an air-conditioning system, there was a ceiling fan that was blowing warm air and there was one common bathroom, which linked the two rooms.

I later went to have a proper look around in the bathroom because one thing that I obviously can't stand to look at in bathrooms is lime scale. But luckily for me the walls were carefully tiled with blue mosaics throughout, which made the bathroom look as if there was a blue lights.

There were two clean towels on the rail, one big toilet roll and two very small-sized toilet soaps.

I did not waste much time before I went in to freshen up. I must have soaked in the bath for quite a while, because by the time I came out of the bathroom, the food that Uncle Bill had ordered earlier on were already brought in for us, and Becky was waiting eagerly for me to come out so that we can eat.

She must have been famished, I could tell from the looks she gave me when I came out from the bathroom.

Before Uncle Bill made the orders for the food, he first of all asked me if I'd like fried rice and chicken. But he was very shocked when I told him that I'd like to eat pounded-yam instead.

"Are you sure you really want to eat pounded-yam?" he asked shockingly.

"Yes, Uncle Bill, I love eating pounded-yam," I told him.

Becky wanted to have it as well, pounded-yam with egusi soup and assorted meat.

"How come you like to eat pounded-yam?" asked Becky.

"Mm, it seems to me as if you're asking me 'How come you're African', I teased. Okay, my dad made sure that we ate one African meal every week and pounded-yam gradually became my favourite. My mum loves it too," I told Becky and Uncle Bill.

"Good, good. So we're all going to eat the same type of food," Uncle Bill said.

"Yes, we're all going to eat the same type of food," Becky repeated.

"Sure," I replied excitedly.

When Uncle Bill had finished ordering the food, he nodded repeatedly with a smile.

I could tell from the expression on his face that he was quite impressed that his brother (my dad) had done a good job bringing me up to like African foods.

I like pounded yam because it's like mashed potato when prepared, it is my favorite from all African foods that I've ever tasted. Although preparing it from the state of raw yam is time consuming. That's why dad prefers to buy the powdered type that is easier to prepare just in the same way that you prepare mashed potato in powder form.

All the same, I've watched my dad prepare the yam once; first he cut the fresh yam into bits and then boiled it until it was properly cooked. He then poured it inside a mortar and then used the pestle to pound it to form dough.

After we'd finish our dinner, I used the phone in our room to try to call Ireland, and I got through to speak with my mum and dad. I was delighted to tell them about my flight and what happened before I finally found Uncle Bill and Becky in the airport, and most importantly that I was fine and starting to enjoy my visit, even though I was only in Lagos city, which meant that the journey had only just begun.

Mum and Dad spoke briefly with Uncle Bill and Becky as well. And later we all settled down to watch an interesting African movie, which was showing on one of the local channels.

CHAPTER SIX
Giant Mosquitoes

When I was a little girl, I used to have nightmares about giant mosquitoes chasing me, reason being that my dad used to tell scary stories about them too often. That used to happen only in my dreams, but having landed in Africa, I thought that I'd come face to face with giant mosquitoes and so I'd come prepared.

I brought out one of the tubes of the mosquito repellent that Mum had bought earlier in Dublin for the purpose of the journey, and had intended to use the entire content of the tube all at one go, as I didn't want to wake up in the morning looking like a scary monster. *I'm going to apply lavishly all over my body before I go to bed*, I thought to myself, as I placed it on the bedside table first to have that little chart which Becky promised me on our way from the airport.

Dad also made jokes about those giant daddy-long leg mosquitoes; those are the types that you see very often during the summer periods. I hate them because you can easily find them hanging around your bedroom walls or in the bathroom when you least expected to see them. Once I found one very gigantic one in my bedroom wall dangling its legs and I almost screamed my head off before Dad came in to get it out.

Dad also used to joke that those gigantic ones were probably stupid because of their huge size and forget to bite you. But the teeny-weenie ones that you find in Africa are so dangerous that they can cause you to have malaria fever if bitten by them, and that was due to their tiny but sensible nature, he'd say.

Whichever way, I knew that mosquitoes generally are dangerous, and I wasn't going to take any chances with them, whether big or small.

Later Uncle Bill took time to explain to me why he happened to be in Lagos city at that point in time, before he retired to sleep in the smaller room after listening to the NTA news at nine o'clock. He didn't come to Lagos city very often, apart from when he came to collect Becky at the end of each term.

Becky lived in Lagos with her mum and step-dad during school terms only, which meant that at the end each school term she went back to the village to spend her holidays. That must have been hectic for her, as she had to keep moving back and forth all the time because the village was quite far away from Lagos city.

On the other hand, Uncle Bill told me that in addition to collecting Becky, he had some other things to do in the city. One of which was about sorting out some paper works in a government department concerning his pension money. According to him, we would have to spend two days more in Lagos city before we can travel down to the village, which I didn't mind personally because I thought I could use the extra days to visit places in Lagos city.

Then it was time for Becky and me to go to sleep, I had to remind her about the promise she made to me earlier in the taxi that she was going to tell me something important. Becky spoke very slowly and she told me that I should try to slower the pace at which I spoke too because she finds my English too fast to follow. However, before she started, she switched off the light in the room and everywhere was nearly dark, apart from the light that was coming from the television set. I wondered if what she wanted to tell had something to do with witches or ghosts, because I was too scared about stuff like that.

I was a bit sceptical, so I asked her why she had the light turned off first of all. She did not give any clear reason, but asked me instead to make her a promise not to tell anyone else about it. I was quite apprehensive at first but thought either way I had nothing to lose.

"Promise me that you'll not tell anyone else about what I'm going to tell you," Becky said.

"Hey, is it some kind of secret?" I asked hastily.

"Yes, kind of," she replied calmly.

"If you've got a confession to make, why don't you go to church and make your confession to the 'father,'" I said teasingly.

"I thought I could trust you, and now you're turning it into a joke," she said rather crossly.

"Is it something very serious? I said. You sound quite angry.

"Yes, it is," she replied.

"Go on then, I'm listening," I said.

"But you have to promise me first," she said, firmly.

Okay then, I cross my heart and hope to die," I said.

"Why do you say that?" Becky asked, looking pretty worried.

"But you wanted me to make you a promise, and that's what I've done now," I replied.

"I know, but you're making it sound like a curse, that's not very good you know. Bad things happen to people when they make dangerous oaths, I've seen it happen many times, and you shouldn't do that for my sake or anyone else's, for any reason whatsoever," she said carefully.

"But it is only a simple promise, I hadn't taken any dangerous oaths," I said.

"Could you please then make your promise in a more simple way?" she said, demandingly.

"Alright, alright, I promise," I said simply.

"That's a lot better," she said, smiling.

With the air-conditioner buzzing on, the room temperature had turned really cool and nice and I loved it that way, but Becky complained bitterly that she was freezing and wrapped herself up with the spare blanket, which we found inside the wardrobe in the small room.

"Can you stay up much longer?" she asked. Because what I'm going to tell you is a very long story," she said.

"What of you Becky? Aren't you tired and sleepy, we can leave this story until tomorrow if you like," I told her.

"It's you that I'm worried about, you've only come from a very long journey," she said.

"Well, that depends, I said. But don't worry about me, I love listening to stories."

"I think it's better for me to forget about it anyway, as this is not in the story category which you're expecting to hear," she said.

"No, I don't mean it like that at all, I said quickly. I love listening to all types of stories. Maybe we can have some peanuts while you're talking if you don't mind, I've loads of them in my bag."

"Alright then, I'll fetch the bottle of soft drink from the fridge," she said.

"Now let's hear about your secret story," I said in a friendly way as I poured out some peanuts into a bowl.

She nodded her head, mumbling softly, 'all right' and then she began to tell her story. It was more of a horror story than just girlie secret stuff.

"My name is Becky as you know already, but it isn't an English name and certainly not the type that you can find in the book of names," she said.

"Don't be daft; there are so many Beckys in my school, moreover it's a lovely name," I told her.

"Not with my type of Becky, it's only shortened from Beki-bele, she explained. And it's in our native dialect." Becky forgot to interpret the meaning to me, and strangely I didn't bother asking either.

"My parents are no longer together as you must have guessed, and my mother has since re-married," she said. "Now I live with my mum and my stepfather here in Lagos during school terms.

"Four years ago when my parents first split up, I decided to go and live with my mum's elder sister, Naomi, because I was shattered by my parent's divorce and I'd hated both of them, and didn't want to live with any of them at the time. So you can imagine my joy when my aunt invited me over to come and live with her in the north," she said.

Becky said also that her aunt travelled all the way from the north to come to the village just for her sake, in order words it was how her aunt made her to believe at the time. She was very happy the day that she left the village with her aunt, because she thought that it was a very good opportunity to escape from her parent's madness. But she soon discovered that her thoughts were wrong; as Aunty Naomi, as she used to call her, had other plans. Becky also told me that her aunt was married to a soldier and they lived in the northern part of the country with their seven children—four boys and three girls.

"It was such a long journey traveling from the east side to the northern part of the country, and by the time we got to our destination, it was so late in the night and the children had all gone to bed," she said. "But I soon saw a tiny face peer out of the window curtains as Aunty Naomi rang the doorbell, and the next thing I knew were shouts and screams of 'mummy—oyo—yo, mummy—oyo—yo' (a joyous cheer of greetings) everywhere."

"And as soon as the door went open, the children all rushed out to welcome their mum, and perhaps me too as I'd thought initially."

Becky was only ten years old at the time and her aunt's eldest daughter, Rebecca, was about the same age. She'd been so delighted to see all her aunt's children because it was the very first time that she saw them, as aunty Naomi hadn't brought any of them with her to the village before.

"Aunty Naomi's husband was very tall and skinny, his complexion was so dark you'd think that he uses diesel oil as his daily body lotion," Becky explained. "And his eyes were so big and red they made him look really scary."

The children all called him *Daddy*, but her aunt called him *Tony*. But she knew that his full name was Anthony anyway. The house had only three bedrooms and one large living area where they entertained guests, all inside a very huge compound, which housed some other families too. All the boys in the house shared one room; the girls in the second room, while aunty Naomi and uncle Tony lived in the third bedroom.

This meant that Becky had to join the girls in their already cramped up bedroom, which made a total of four girls altogether, sharing in one room.

Becky said she knew immediately that trouble was starting to brew when she said goodnight to both her aunty and Uncle Tony (as she called him) but he did not bother to reply her.

"Go with Rebecca when you've finished eating your food okay, and I'll see you in the morning," Aunty Naomi had said to her as she and uncle Tony stood up to leave the living room that night.

"Goodnight, Aunty Naomi and Uncle Tony,' she'd happily said to both of them.

"My aunt replied by saying goodnight, but skinny bones Uncle Tony never said a word. And I knew instantly that trouble was brewing up already," Becky said.

Becky paused soon to take a deep breath before continuing, which made me also suggest to her once more that we take a break if she was feeling tired of talking. She looked intently at me for while, and asked if I was the one feeling tired so she could stop and carry on the next morning.

I confessed to her that I'd been feeling a bit sleepy before she started to talk, but since she'd began telling her story, I wasn't feeling sleepy any longer, as I was really into it.

"Thank you Sandra," she said, smiling half-heartedly.

"What for?" I asked.

"I hope I'm not beginning to bore you; it's just that there really isn't anything interesting about all of this, they're full of sad and painful memories," Becky said, and immediately I noticed a sad expression on her face, as if she wanted a little cry.

"You're not obliged to continue if you don't want to," I said.

"Of course, I know that." She answered." There is one part of the story that I hadn't dared reveal to anyone before, which I'm prepared to tell you tonight, and that was the reason I asked you to make that promise in the first place."

I sensed that she had a lot more coming and kind of prepared myself for any shocking revelations.

"I went through a number of horrifying situations while living with Aunty Naomi, but nothing was as bad as what happened to me in the end before I decided to run away," she said.

"You ran away?" I asked, shockingly.

"I'd probably be dead by now if I hadn't run away. I couldn't bear the sufferings anymore," she replied.

"And are you sure that you're ready to share it with me now?" I asked calmly, as I prepared myself to hear what Becky was going to say next.

"Yes, I'm willing to share it with you tonight if you let me, because I just might not feel the same way when I wake up tomorrow morning about all this," Becky replied, adjusting her seating position.

"By all means, go on. I want to hear it," I said, sensing that she was very prepared to let out all secrets that she's been hiding for so long. Whatever it was, she was set to get it off her chest in order to free her mind and face her future like a proper teenager, and not allow herself to get bogged down with unfortunate situations that weren't her fault in the first place. And I too was very prepared to give her the chance.

Meanwhile I poured more drink into her glass. She took one more sip from the glass and a deep breath and then continued with her story.

"Rebecca told me on that first night that there wasn't anymore sleeping space in the bed, and that I should manage to sleep on the mat, and then threw a tattered mat at my face," said Becky. "You know what? I might have been living in the village since I was born, but before then, I hadn't slept bare on a mat before, let alone a tattered one. And since there was no other alternative open to me, I humbly spread the mat on the floor and lay down to sleep on it," Becky said sadly.

Becky also said that her aunt's daughter Rebecca instructed her to fold the mat and store it away under the bed when she woke up first thing the next morning. "That first night was horrible, she said. I couldn't sleep very well as all I did was toss and turn until very early the next morning when Rebecca tried to wake me up to join her to go and fetch water from the rocks, which was miles and miles away. But as a result from not sleeping very well in the night, I'd been very sleepy still and kept on drifting back to sleep until she shouted out my name really loud, to get up immediately and stop wasting her time. I managed to sit up on the mat, which was to serve as my bed for the rest period of my stay in my aunt's house, as I stammered a 'g-good m-morning' and told Rebecca to give me a minute to change from my nightgown into something else, but Rebecca reacted very badly to my request to take off my nightdress first as though I asked her to give me a million dollars from her." Continued Becky.

"Even then, my troubles were only beginning to unfold, as

JOURNEY OF THE IRISH CHILD

she pointed out that she was only leading me to the rocks in order to show me how to get there myself alone next time, as neither she nor anyone else in the household would ever go with me to fetch water," Becky said to me.

Becky thought initially that Rebecca being around the same age as her might bring the two of them together as best buddies and possibly do things together, but her thoughts were completely wrong. Rebecca made it very clear from the first day that she wasn't welcomed to their home.

"How naive I'd been, thinking that Aunt Naomi was on my side, but she was my aunt you know; however, I only realised how wrong I was when I tried to protest a little and complain about Rebecca's attitudes towards me and my aunt was not prepared to defend me in anyway. Rather, I made everything worse for myself; because Aunty Naomi did not waste time to give me a dirty slap across my face was soon as Rebecca informed her of my unwillingness to go and fetch the water alone.

"The moment that I realised that Rebecca was treated as a little princess around the house and was somehow untouchable, I relented and from that day forward, I became the little slave girl of my aunt's evil kingdom. Everyone snapped at me at the slightest opportunity, from dawn to dusk, it was always 'Becky come and do this, or come and do that.' I cooked, washed and scrubbed the floors every day, and I wasn't allowed to go school either," Becky explained sadly.

"That must have been awful, having to do all the chores by yourself without any help from anyone," I told Becky.

"Many times I wished that they sent me back to my parents, even though they were no longer together, and I also knew that I would be subjected to move back and forth between my parents like a homeless tramp, but that didn't bother me anymore because in my mind, I'd already forgiven my parents for splitting up, after all I wasn't the only one whose parents were divorced and if all the other kids coped with their parents' separations, somehow I could deal with it as well," said Becky moodily.

She regretted however that, had she forgiven her mum and dad earlier, she wouldn't have landed herself into that horrible situation in the first place, because there wouldn't have been any other reason that would have caused her to go and live with her Aunty Naomi up north.

"I couldn't understand how my once kind-hearted aunt suddenly changed into a horror monster. She allowed her husband and children to treat me so badly and order me around the house without showing any concern," Becky said regrettably as her eyes started brimming over with tears.

Becky said that, she despised seeing her uncle Tony early in the mornings and tried to avoid staring into his oily red eyes, but that was unavoidable as he would call her and then bark orders at her every morning like she was one of his new army recruits.

"It must have been a dreadful period for you Becky," I said. "But your aunt shouldn't have allowed that, because that is bullying," I told Becky.

"Forget about Aunty Naomi, she could not take her own stand; her evil genius husband dictated everything she did. She never challenged him once, not even for her children."

"One fine morning, as I woke up to the sweet whispers of the birds, and rushed to the kitchen to begin my daily chores, I overheard Uncle Tony and my aunt talking about me in the living room. Uncle Tony was hammering that I wasn't doing enough and if my aunt could not make me do more chores then he would have to use military force to make me do more," Becky said.

"I hope he didn't at any time physically beat you up, did he?" I asked, feeling so sorry for her.

"Yes, he did, many times he used his koboko to whip me," she replied.

"You don't mean it, and you didn't call in the police. By the way, what is koboko?" I asked.

"Um, I'm not very sure how to explain it to you." She grinned shyly. "And about calling the police, I didn't find the need to."

"I'm not blaming you, but I think that you should have tried to get to the police. You should have made your aunt and her husband pay for mistreating you," I said.

"Let' just forget about that part okay? It's no use," she said.

"If you say so, I think I know what it is," I said. "It must be a type of horsewhip that soldiers usually use in training grounds to enforce discipline. I mean the koboko stuff."

"Yeah, you got it," Becky agreed. "Anyway, like I was saying, I rushed back into our bedroom and lay back on my mat and covered my head with my tattered piece of cover-cloth for a few minutes, thinking about what I'd overheard Uncle Tony telling my aunt and I thought as I cried that morning, *Here I am working my head off, yet the giraffe-necked-daytime-witch thinks that I'm not doing enough, and yet he doesn't know how to inculcate discipline into the empty skulls of his own children.*

"I found it hard to get up to do more chores after hearing Uncle Tony speak so ill of me, but Aunty Naomi soon began yelling my name. She yelled so loud, anyone outside could hear her, except her lazy children," she said.

Just then as Becky finished her last statement, Uncle Bill interrupted us; he woke up to go to the bathroom, although he didn't come into our room and so we were able to carry on. He must have been dog-tired to worry about Becky and I being awake that late.

"You must have felt very lonely, but that wasn't right, especially your aunt allowing her husband and children to bully you around. Pity you didn't call the police," I said calmly and handed some tissues to Becky to wipe her face as she started to weep suddenly.

Typically, there wouldn't have been the need for Becky to go to the police as she said earlier, it wasn't as if they would believe her story, besides, the police too would have thought exactly like most people who lived in their compound, that her Aunty Naomi and Uncle Tony were only giving her what they saw as proper upbringing because none of them saw it as child abuse. "I couldn't figure out the reason why they treated me so cruelly. I wondered most times if it was possible that my aunt was angry with my father for divorcing her sister and decided to take it out on me."

"That was clearly not your fault and, moreover, they still didn't have the right to mistreat you the way that they did for whatever reason," I told Becky.

"Sandy! Sandy! From the way you speak, I quite agree with everyone that you're an intelligent girl, you know, from the way that you talk and everything. And I wish you were there in my aunt's house when they were maltreating me, I'm sure that you could have successfully talked sense into their brainless heads in that crazy house of commotion. I'm sure they would've changed from all their negative attitudes towards me," Becky told me as her face showed a cheerful expression for once since we started talking.

"Thanks for exaggerating like everyone else, Becky," I said. "You're the most intelligent and brave person that I've seen, else you wouldn't be here to tell your story after going through so much cruelty at such a young age at the hands of those you called family," I told Becky.

"Very well, Sandra, you are exaggerating now, because I wasn't that brave like you want to believe," Becky replied.

"Yes, you were, and you still are," I told her.

"No, I wasn't, and still am not," she said.

"Yes you were, and I must say that you are very lucky to be alive today, because I've heard many ugly stories about young children been maltreated to their death," I said quite frankly.

"I haven't even told you that I was at many times starved of food as well, and with empty stomach I'd walk the long distance under the burning sun to fetch water to fill two big drums, it got to a point when I began to bald in the centre of my head and I thought that I was going to die anyway," Becky said, forcing a laugh.

"You're kidding me," I said. "That was so cruel, you shouldn't laugh about it. You didn't deserve to be treated like that by your aunt or any other person for matter, not even your own parents have the right to mistreat you so wickedly. They could both end up in prison if that happened in Ireland you know," I said furiously.

"Yeah, but unfortunately, here isn't Ireland where children's rights are well-protected," Becky said regrettably.

"I agree with you," I said sympathetically.

"So how did you manage to escape from your aunt's evil kingdom?" I asked.

"Sorry I haven't quite finished yet, I'm going to tell you everything about that now and I hope that I'll feel better afterwards: I not only did chores around the home, but used to go hawking in the streets as well you know," Becky began with a pretentious smile on her face.

"You mean like those kids we saw in the traffic on our way from the airport?" I asked, shocked.

"Yes." She nodded. "And since then, whenever I see children out on the street hawking, it brings back hurtful memories. When certain things happen to you, they don't go away, they stay with you and torment you all your life," she said.

"No matter what they are, if and when you're prepared to let it go, it does. You might not forget it, but you go past it and they cannot hurt you anymore. You are doing so well," I said. "And you'll get past it in the end. I promise."

"What exactly do you want to do when you graduate from school?" Becky asked unexpectedly.

"Why?" I queried.

"I don't know, but I think that counselling suits you," she said, grinning. "I think you'll make a perfect one because you're such a inspirational talker."

CHAPTER SEVEN
Horrible History

Something really, really horrible happened to Becky later; however, it afforded her to opportunity to escape from her aunt's enslavement.

"Aunty Naomi and uncle Tony wanted to host a big party for some friends and preparations had already started a week in advance, and my aunt promised me that I must be in my best behaviour in front of the guests on the day of the party, and that I also must wear a new dress," Becky said.

Becky's aunt had been very wicked really. Strangers were coming to the house and she wanted Becky to appear as if she was a happy girl and everything was fine. Though she'd been very happy that she was going to have a new dress, it would be her very first new dress since she arrived at her aunt's house. Her aunt made it quite clear to her that if she really wanted that new dress, she'd have to work extra hard to turn in some good profit from hawking yams in the streets. Becky thought that she didn't have a problem with that. After all, she'd gotten so used to hawking the yams before and had never complained or felt reluctant about going out to sell. She thought that all she had to do was put in more effort and she'd be compensated in the end with a brand new dress for her aunt's party.

"I'd never been so eager to sell as many yams as possible, only I didn't know that it was going to be different this time. Something horrible lay ahead for me, but how was I supposed to know?

"That warm evening, I arranged the yam tubers in the wide tray, which I'd used often to sell yams, and I'd been very, very enthusiastic and was prepared to go through and beyond the routes that I was already familiar with. With the tray full of yams on my head 'Buy your yams' 'Buy your yams' I started calling out to possible buyers, but they were very unlikely. There were no customers anywhere," she explained sadly.

"What would happen if you didn't sell?" I asked, interrupting.

"Mm, I hated thinking about the possibility of not selling at all as that would infuriate my aunt so much, and could result in me having to serve more punishments," she replied.

With those words, Becky closed her eyes, twisted her face, and the agony inside her was almost visible. I knew then that what was coming wasn't going to be pleasant. Becky was fighting hard to hold back the tears, but she soon burst out crying very loudly, If Uncle Bill hadn't been too tired, he would have been woken by the noise. It was time for the bombshell, she's been dancing around it for so long, the time had come that she couldn't keep it in anymore.

"It wasn't my fault, it wasn't my fault, I was only trying my best to sell the yams so that I could get the new dress, which my aunt promised me," she said repeatedly as she started to weep.

Becky was only a child, and she seemed to have gone through many difficulties in life already. The pain and sadness that she expressed was so unbearable, all the things she said made me feel almost like they were happening physically to me. I imagined that it was beyond terrible what she went through.

"No, it wasn't your fault, Becky," I said, attempting to comfort her even when she hadn't really told me what was making her moan so bitterly.

She soon opened her eyes and then wiped her face once again with a part of the dress she was wearing. "I'm so sorry, I didn't mean to break down in front of you like this," she apologised in a whispery voice.

"You don't have to apologise for anything, you're doing the right thing, Becky. Get it out from your mind and you'll feel a lot better," I said, urging her to carry on with whatever there was remaining for her to say.

"Thanks, Sandra," she said softly.

"What are you thanking me for?" I asked.

"Your kind patience," Becky said, and then continued.

"I don't understand why no one wanted to buy any yams on that gloomy day, I believe the day was cursed for my sake."

Nonetheless, Becky persisted in spite of not finding any buyer. But you know, as a small girl, the weight of the yams soon began to get too heavy on her head. And it was also started to affect her neck seriously and she became too tired to continue. Not withstanding the consequences that might befall her should she go back to her aunt's house without making a single sale, she turned to go back home.

As she walked dejectedly towards home, a voice suddenly called out to her, asking her to bring the yams. She looked around to see where the voice was coming from. "Over here, over here." A young man waved from an upstairs balcony across the road, and she also shouted back to the young man to hold on and wait for her, that she was coming.

"That instant I felt a sudden surge of happiness that I might at least be able to make one sale and not receive too much punishment from my aunt."

"I then hurried quickly over to the supposed buyer's front door, and as I knocked he opened the door immediately, flashing an irrelevant smile at me, although I recognised his monkey face."

"'Do you want to buy my yams?' I asked him. And then in turn, he enquired about the cost for each one of the yams, and when I told him what t price it was for the individual yams, he said that he would buy them all.

"I thought that I had suddenly received a miracle from heaven, after walking up and down the roads for such a long time, desperately looking for a buyer and here was this man out of the blue all of a sudden and wanting to buy all of the yams. I couldn't believe it, and I really thought that the offer was too good to be real," she said.

Becky told me that at that point, things began to turn ugly for her, because as the buyer calculated the total cost of the yams and handed the money to Becky, he also asked her to offload all the yam tubers in the corner of his living room, which she agreed without hesitation. It wasn't the first time that she was selling to someone in his or her own homes, including the young man. He was one of her regular customers and she had no cause not to trust him this time around. Unfortunately, as she packed the yams out of the tray, the man quickly closed the door and turned the keys and then grabbed her from behind.

"I was horrified I started to cry, begging him to let me go but he wouldn't. I tried to get out of his strong grip, but he was too strong, he, he…"

Becky broke down again and began to sob, her head bowed in both hands. She needn't say any more because I already knew what the rest of the story was going to be. That evil man who pretended to be the Good Samaritan who wanted to buy all her yams raped her. I felt so bad and wanted to cry with her, but I also felt that it wasn't the best thing to do at that point, because first of all she had just purged a sad secret that she'd been keeping to herself, and needed some comforting. I had to be strong to be able to comfort her, and moreover, it wasn't going to erase all the bad things that happened, if I cried.

When you suddenly discover that someone that you care about has been through so much, the best that you can do is to show some form of kindness at least to let them know that you sympathise with him or her. And that was exactly what I did for Becky.

"I'm really sorry, it must have been so terrifying for you," I told her as I cuddled her to myself, letting her cry a little before giving her a small handkerchief to dry her tears.

"I thought that he was going to kill me, I felt so alone in the entire world, because no one seemed to hear my crying and shouting," Becky said bitterly, nearly quivering.

"And you have kept this to yourself all this time?" I asked.

"Yes," she nodded

"Maybe your aunt and her husband may well have had that maniac put to jail if you'd told them what he did to you," I said.

Becky stared at me, and then she asked if I knew what she did afterwards.

"No, what did you do?" I asked, looking distraughtly at her.

"I felt totally disgusted and ravaged afterwards and threw the money which he'd paid for the yams back at him and staggered out of the flat, but half way down the stairs, I changed my mind and went back to the flat," said Becky. "Luckily for me, the evil monster still laid there on the same spot looking motionless like an overfed crocodile."

"What did you go back for? Weren't you too afraid?" I asked.

"This might seem such a foolish decision, but I wasn't thinking clearly at the time, and somehow I felt like I'd suddenly been possessed by a stronger force, all the fears and pain had disappeared and I didn't waste anytime, I grabbed the money from the floor and dashed out of the flat as quick as possible," she said, half smiling.

JOURNEY OF THE IRISH CHILD

"Tell me you didn't. That was such a bad idea, he could have taken hold of you a second time," I said hastily to her.

"Yes I did, but then as I walked towards home, I changed my mind one more time, and instead of heading back to my aunt's house, I decided to run away with the money. I felt awful taking the money, she said. "But I'd been completely enveloped by this strange feeling, which made feel like I could do anything at that moment.

"Seriously speaking, if there was some kind of weapon in sight at that point, I don't know what I'd have done to that monster or even to myself," she said.

Becky thought that she'd had just enough from going away with her aunt, and perhaps it was time for her to go home, and since she didn't see any other opening for her to do that, she thought it better to run away to the village to be with her parents. She went straight to look for the bus terminus, which she had no idea how to get there, but somehow she was able to get down there with the help of another little girl who was probably more conversant with the environment than she was.

She knew also that she need not waste time unnecessarily because if she didn't go home soon enough her aunt would start looking for her, and if caught what would happen to her was better left to be imagined. It was a risk and she knew it.

"I thought that no matter all the bad things that had happened to me these past two years, I'd put it behind me and go back to my parents, I'd had enough cruelty living with Aunty Naomi, and I wasn't going to allow no one to hurt me any more," said Becky.

"Good spirit," I commended.

"Yeah, and that thought helped me go through it," Becky said. "I bought some bread to eat because I was so hungry by the time I got to the bus station, and then used the remaining money to pay for the fare. The money wasn't even enough but a kind couple completed my fare, when I told them what happened to me."

"Bless that couple," I said, interrupting.

"I knew that some people inside the big coach looked at me like I was some kind of a weirdo because I looked so haggard, but I didn't let that bother me.

The bus didn't waste too much time loading; it was full soon with passengers, and we drove throughout the night and by morning we'd arrived safely," Becky said, this time with a triumphant smile.

"Well done!" I said, praising her courage and effort in telling the story in the first place. And as she came to the end of the story, sadness and anger vanished, her face glowed in ebony black, and she looked so beautiful. I admired her bravery and I told her that what she'd done tonight was the way forward to freeing herself really from a sad and unhappiness through to a brighter side of her future which she had every right to look forward to.

"Thank you so much for being so patient and listening to me, I'm already feeling better now that I've purged out everything," she said happily.

"I think that you should have told your mum and your dad about what you went through because it wasn't your fault, and besides it's still not too late to tell them about it," I told Becky.

"I don't know, I felt terrible and thought that perhaps it was somehow my fault, and if I told anyone I might further be looked upon dreadfully with so much hatred and be treated like an outcast, or something." She sighed.

"Your parents deserve to know about all the things that you've been through, both at the hands of your aunt and that wicked monster. I'm sure they'll understand. It wasn't your fault at all, and so you have to try and talk to one of your parents about it," I said, persuasively.

In the end Becky told me that she wasn't yet ready to tell her mum and Uncle Bill, but promised to think about the possibility later. However, I discovered that her urge to tell me about her story was triggered by my early reaction concerning those little kids that we saw hawking along the road on our way from the airport. She'd been there; she understood what it was like to be out there and she also knew, that very bad and horrible plights befall many innocent children as they go about looking for customers to buy their wares in the streets. And above all, she also knew that some of those kids were forced to be out there, against their wish, possibly because of so much poverty in their homes or they were living with a wicked distant relative who'd forced them into the twenty-first-century slavery.

CHAPTER EIGHT
Who Cares Anyway!

I'd completely forgotten to use the mosquito repellent before falling asleep last night after Becky and I finished talking. I'd been too absorbed in Becky's story and did not remember about the possible dangers of not using the mosquito repellent to protect my skin before going to bed. Thankfully though, there wasn't a single mosquito bite on my skin in the morning, perhaps the window net prevented the mosquitoes from getting inside the room and, besides, the cold air from the air-conditioner must also have rendered any of them that could been inside the room already inactive.

Who cares anyway? Mosquitoes have not invaded me and that is all that matters, the only thought that came to my mind when I went inside the bathroom to look at myself in the mirror first thing the next morning and saw that my face was at clear of measles —like spots.

The next day started brilliant with the sun already out shining so early in the morning. Uncle Bill woke up really early to prepare for the appointment regarding his pensions in the "Ministry of Finance," as he referred to it. However, before he left the hotel that morning, he tried to find out from me if I knew whether it was just as difficult in Ireland to secure a pension upon retirement.

But just as you might guess, I knew nothing absolutely about pensions and I told him just that, even though I was well aware that back in Ireland, my nana herself was a pensioner. But that doesn't guarantee that I have to be an expert on the subject or any other for that matter. And moreover, that kind of stuff was far too complicated for my age anyway. But I still wanted the conversation to continue more or less. I strongly feel that it was important for me that I tried my best to get to know my new relatives, you know, there was still so much to find out about my dad's family, how they live, or how they view the rest of the world from their own perspective. I have only spent one night with only Uncle Bill and Becky, yet I've learnt a lot and heard a lot about what goes on with my people. Of course, they are my people even though I still hadn't met them all or so to speak, that cab driver that carried us from the airport suggested to Uncle Bill that I be taught or informed about everything. Well, no one person can learn too much in just a few days, but the point is that I am determined to find out just about anything that would benefit me in the cause of this journey, and it is never too late to start.

I deliberately started an entirely different topic, as I didn't know anything whatsoever about pensions, and had therefore not contributed anything.

I told Uncle Bill that I could tell him something different, at first I didn't quite have any subject matter readily in mind, and after searching my mind for a while I just mentioned mortgage, it sort of came out from my mouth unexpectedly. Um, I didn't even know how or where to begin, and my eyes were now shining like that of a petty thief who had been caught in the act. Becky glanced briefly at me and I kind of winked at her for no obvious reasons, but Uncle Bill was now listening and waiting for me to start the conversation, or at least tell him something about what I'd just mentioned.

Not that I knew so much about it in the first place, my dad usually said to me "always bite only what you can chew" my dad likes to speak to me in parables most of the time, and he prides himself in it. Not that he spoke in parables to the parents of his 'little angels' at the hospital else they wouldn't understand his a single thing when he tries to explain some prescriptions to them.

Actually the funniest part about this whole parable thing is that my dad's father used to do exactly the same thing. I think it's a good thing to pass on certain gifts from one generation to the other, but this thing about speaking in parables isn't the best of gifts and I really detest taking over from my dad and I pray its not one of those *from one generation to the next generation type of thing*, because I'm not the type that would like to get my own kids confused with some kind of coded language. Although it would be a lot better if it was the Nigerian ' broken English' stuff.

Once my dad said something to me in parable, you know, when someone says to a child to make sure that she is blind when all those kisses scenes start to pop up on the screen of the telly. I just stared at my dad motionless like a zombie after he said it, you'll know what I'm talking about if you've ever been to a church where the congregations are speaking in tongues and you're the only person who doesn't seem to understand. Without any warning, I just blabbed out to my dad "do you mean that I should blind my eyes whenever I saw two people kissing in the telly?" I was about eleven years old then, and I'm not so sure that you want to hear about my dad's response to my question. He just laughed at my naivety and said that at eleven, he knew I was still in dreamland or else I was suppose to understand the meaning of what he said, but sorry I wasn't a magician either.

However, I knew that I had really messed up this time, my dad would have told me that I had obviously 'bitten more than I could chew' because I had giving myself the obligation to explain what mortgage was to Uncle Bill and he was very anxious to hear about it as is if he truly hadn't heard nothing about that word before.

Now I've realised how important it is to always be very attentive in class when you're taken lessons, because you never know when you'll need to put what you've learnt in your class to practice, or in other words, prove how intelligent you really are in school. I'm the only student in my class who never did very well in business studies, and this was one chance for me to show that I've been a good student.

I've learnt a few things about mortgage in school, and I've also heard Mum and Dad talking about it many times in the past, mostly about repaying the mortgage on our house. Well, I had to say something and as I continued to talk about it, surprisingly though, I discovered that Uncle Bill knew nothing at all about the subject and so I still carried the day. But more shocking to me was that Uncle Bill was a head teacher in many primary schools around their community for so many years before, and I thought in that circumstance he'd be a bit more enlightened than most people who lived in the village.

In the end, I had to do the *head-teacher* stuff. You know, one explanation after the other just to make him understand what I was talking about. Still lying on the bed and covered in blankets because the air-condition system had been very cooling in the early morning, I patiently explained to Uncle Bill essentially what I understood about mortgage.

He seemed dumbfounded when I explained to him that someone could take out a mortgage on his or her house, you know, a loan that you use your house as security or collateral if you like, and it also means that a person who is buying a property for the first time doesn't have to have the money to pay for the full cost of the property, because the mortgage company arranges to pay out the entire amount on behalf of the buyer, and then…

Uncle Bill took a very deep breath and said all of a sudden, "Umm, no wonder, no wonder!" he said in a way that made me to discontinue with what I was saying, to find out why he said that, and in such a tone of frustration.

"No wonder for what, Uncle Bill?" I asked in a low tone of voice.

"Now I know why some people in the western world are so lazy," he replied, shaking his head disapprovingly.

"Excuse me, what are you talking about, Uncle Bill?" I questioned, not following what he had said.

"Wait a minute! Are you telling me that you can buy a house without paying for it with your own money?" he asked, confused.

"Yes, Uncle Bill, you only have to pay a small percentage and the mortgage company does the rest on your behalf. But first you must show some kind of proof that you are capable of paying back to the mortgage company, and that is known as proving your income, well you'll also be expected to meet up with some other conditions too, as the case may be," I said.

"What happens after that?" he questioned.

"Like I was saying, then the total cost of the house is spread into so many years, and you're then required to start repayment of a certain amount of money to the mortgage company every month until the full amount is cleared," I explained.

"This reminds me, your father wrote to me two years ago that he bought a house, does it mean also that a mortgage company paid for the house for him?" Uncle Bill asked seriously.

"I suppose so, that is quite obvious," I replied slowly.

"I don't believe this, said Uncle Bill furiously. Why didn't your father explain to me clearly that he was only a tenant to some mortgage company?" he queried. "I was so proud at the time when he told me the news about this lovely new house that he'd bought in the city of Dublin. You have no idea how much I bragged about the news to everyone in the village. Family members gathered for a small party, and you're now telling me that my brother doesn't even own the house."

"Don't take it wrongly, Uncle Bill, the house belongs to my dad as long as he continues to keep up the re-payments," I said.

"What happens when he stops paying back to the mortgage company?" he questioned further.

"My dad works very hard so that won't happen, but if it does happen eventually, there is always only one outcome. The mortgage company will repossess the house," I answered.

"Repossess, you mean take it back? No wonder your father cannot take out time to visit his aged parents, every year he promises and never fulfils his promise to come. I guess I understand now, but what a shame. It's just as if we've lost him completely to the western world," Uncle Bill lamented bitterly.

"Don't talk like that about my dad, he's a hard-working man and that's the reason why he hadn't the chance to come and visit you guys," I said.

"Guys, you mean 'me' guys?" he snapped.

"Oh, Uncle Bill!! Don't be d…" I had to stop the sentence midway before committing a serious offence of foul-mouthed, because if I'd completed the sentence *don't be daft* it would have turned out a different ball game, I mean if he was furious because I said the word *guys* to him, and giving what happened in the airport between him and that teenager.

Yeah, you might think that, so what's wrong in saying *guys* to an uncle? Big deal, I'd say, as far as my dad's culture is concerned, because that means one thing generally to the people of my dad's culture. It means EXTREME RUDENESS. My dad pointed out that it's a serious act of disregard in Africa for children to say things like *don't be silly*, or *don't be stupid* to a grown up as they consider it offensive. And although he is now used to all the casual way that kids interact with everybody including their own parents, he stressed that it was a bit odd for him when he first came to Ireland to see how children were very playful around grown up adults, unlike in his hometown where young children almost don't have anything in common with their elders apart from respecting them all the time. Dad also used to say that as a child, he almost never spoke when his dad was present, or he almost quivers when his dad talked to him, except on very special occasions, which was rare to come by. However he believes that it is very important that children learn how to respect and obey their elders from an early age so that they too will grow up to become responsible adults later in life.

"Were you trying to tell me something, Sandra?" asked Uncle Bill.

"No, not really, I was only trying to tell you that I didn't mean to be rude when I mentioned the word 'guys, it was only a slip of tongue," I said.

"Whatever you say, he said. I shouldn't be too surprised after all I know how all these *oyinbo* children behaves. Anyway that is over now. But one more thing though, what is the meaning of 'proving your income?'" he asked.

"Don't you know what it means to prove your income, Uncle Bill?" I giggled.

"Becky suddenly burst out laughing uncontrollably.

"Don't you want to know why I'm laughing so much?" she asked, amused.

"Why?" Uncle Bill asked unceremoniously.

"Yeah, what's so funny?" I asked demandingly.

"Papa, Becky called to Uncle Bill. It is very funny that you don't understand anything that Sandra says, and come to think of it that you were a head-teacher for many years. So how come you seem not to understand simple things?" Becky asked, still reeling in laughter.

"Don't you know that it is very rude to laugh at your father's mistakes? I think this city is spoiling you, perhaps I should keep you a bit longer in the village this time," Uncle Bill said snappily to Becky, sounding quite embarrassed.

"I'm sure she didn't mean to sound so offensive, Uncle Bill, she's probably joking, aren't you Becky?" I said calmly, trying to ease Uncle Bill's uncomfortable mood.

"You're very polite, Sandra, I hope that Becky learns one or two things from you about proper manners," Uncle Bill said, forgetting what he said earlier about the behaviours of the *oyinbo* children. *I'm sure this proves to him that the upbringing or good behaviours of any particular child doesn't really depend on where he or she was born.* I thought silently with a naughty smile.

"Sorry, Papa," Becky apologised.

"Well, let me tell the two you something that is very important, said Uncle Bill. The quality of education in my days was a lot better compared to what you people have nowadays."

"How do you mean," I questioned.

"Can you imagine that school children nowadays are allowed to carry calculators with them into the classrooms? Sometimes I wonder what is going to happen with the children of the next generation," he bemoaned.

"So what's wrong in using calculators in the classroom, Uncle Bill?" I asked.

"Yeah, what's wrong in that, Papa?" Becky added.

"In those days, you only had to search and scratch your head and brain until you found a way to solve your mathematics by your own effort; therefore in my own opinion, using a calculator inside the classroom is nothing but cheating and it shouldn't be allowed," he fumed.

"Anyway, you're entitled to your opinion, Uncle Bill, and moreover using a calculator or computers in school makes learning much fun," I argued.

"Great, let's debate and see who wins. Should calculators be allowed in classrooms or not? Don't worry I'll be the judge," Becky said, sarcastically.

"Sorry, but I don't have the time for any stupid contest this early morning. I've got to hurry for my appointment," Uncle Bill said as he struggles to tie the laces of his old shoes, anyone could tell that those shoes had seen their better days, but Uncle Bill didn't seem to mind at all.

"It will be so boring in school if everything remained like they were in the olden days," I said.

"I suppose you're right," Uncle Bill agreed in the end.

"That's better," replied Becky.

"Anyway, calculators or not, I don't like maths subject anyway," I said.

"Maths is my best subject, but I dislike geography. I don't like talking about things that really doesn't exist, and you need to see my geo teacher in action. I mean when she is in class; she gets very serious teaching the subject as though her life depends on it. But you know what, that didn't change the way I feel about the subject one bit," Becky said.

"And what are these things which you guys talk about in class that you feel do not exist?" I asked Becky curiously.

"You know, all those things like tornados, twisters and the rest of them," she replied.

"Rest of what?" I asked, confused.

"Mm, I'm talking about stuff like snow and volcanic eruptions," Becky replied, looking uncertain.

"Do you seriously believe that these things that you mentioned doesn't exist really?" I queried.

"Well, I'm not exactly saying that they don't exist, the only reason why I said so is because I don't see any of those things in this country, and for that reason it bores me to study about them in class. In reality, I know that they exist and I've seen on television how towns and cities are sometimes wrecked by them," Becky said.

"And have you always wished that some of these things that you mentioned happened here in this country so that you may like geography?" I asked her seriously.

"That's a dumb question to ask. Who prays for doomsday anyway? The subjects simply bores me to death, that's all," Becky replied nonchalantly.

Since neither Becky or I looked set to go out, Uncle Bill had to leave us behind in the hotel, but with a promise to come back early to take us out. Later the two of us went to have our breakfast in the restaurant, which was located on the ground floor of the hotel. I ordered fried eggs and sausages with toast, while Becky ordered exactly the same except the eggs. (She hates egg yolks for some reason.)

I bought two cans of cold orange juice after breakfast and then we strolled around the gate outside the hotel. The hotel looked really posh from the outside apart from the excess dust that was flying everywhere, which made the building look like an old missionary temple. Anyway, we only roamed around enough time for the hotel-maids to clean our rooms, though it was still lovely——the walk I mean.

The room had been sprayed with a good air spray, and the air conditioner made everywhere so relaxed. Even the toilet smelt good. And guess what? Becky said she used to watch *Fear Factor* and *The Lost World* at home. They had a satellite dish too. There was a foreign movie showing on one of the channels, but I preferred to watch the local channel. I loved the traditional movies.

It was reaching midday and Becky and I were expecting Uncle Bill to come back any moment to take us out to go and see some of the city's nicest places. Because while Becky and I were out strolling around the hotel complex earlier, she told me that there was more to the city than seeing children hawking in the streets. In fact, she boosted that I hadn't seen anything yet, because there are the posh side of the city like Ikoyi, Victoria Island, Ikeja, Suru-Lere, Maryland, Festac Town and so on. 'Wow' I said when she started mentioning all these names. To me they all sounded like the names of places in a fairyland, only that these posh places are actually there in

Lagos city, but reserved only for the elite, you know, the rich and famous people of the most populous State in the country. 'That's not fair' you might think. But these are very expensive areas of the city for anyone to live and you don't expect the less fortunate people, who're struggling to feed their family to be able to afford the luxury of living in such high places. But you know what, I didn't really take that as a serious problem because even in countries like America, London, Paris, Germany or Ireland and elsewhere in the western world too, the very rich and powerful people lived mostly in choice areas.

However, I was very excited and couldn't wait for uncle bill to arrive at the door so we can go out, I was very eager to see all those lovely places.

I asked Becky if her dad who lived only in the village knew the city well enough to know where he was taking us. Becky wasn't sure about it.

"As you know, my father doesn't live in this city. I'm very sure he knows a lot of places, but we can ask questions anyway. For me, I've only been to the Apapa Amusement Park and the famous Bar-Beach," she said.

"Wow! I exclaimed. Sounds interesting," I said. "But is that a large park and does it have swings and a merry-go-round and stuff like that?"

"Sure," Becky answered, and then started to go on about how lovely the park was.

"Swings, like for younger kids you mean?" I asked, not so impressed.

"Isn't that what you're talking about?" she asked, grinning.

Becky and I got so bored waiting for Uncle Bill's return, and by the time he finally got back to the hotel, it was almost too late to go anywhere far away. Uncle Bill chartered a cab to take us to the Apapa Amusement Park, which was very close to our hotel. But again we only got there as the main gate was been shut for the day. The security guy whose look was sure to scare anyone away told us politely to return early the following day, so I didn't get to see the city, and even had a chance in the most famous amusement park in the city. *Hard Luck* you'd say.

I kept my cool throughout the journey back to the hotel even though I was disappointed; however, Becky didn't take it lightly with her dad as she nagged for the rest of the evening. One good thing, though, Uncle Bill was successful with the meeting about his pensions, except that he had to report back the next day to finalise everything. He assumed that my visit brought him the good luck this time after shuttling to and fro between the city and the village without luck in the past.

However, he promised us happily that he'd make it up to Becky and I the next day after his concluding meetings in the ministry.

Hopefully, we would be going out together in the morning and then, after Uncle Bill's meeting, we'll proceed from there to the very famous Bar-Beach.

CHAPTER NINE
Sunshine

There was a very heavy downpour in the night, which lasted through until the early hours of the morning, it was so heavy, and I'd not experienced rain accompanied with so much noise before. The sounds of thunderstorm were like the roars of an approaching tsunami, and then there were the noises of raindrops, which sounded as if people were pouring dry sands on the rooftop.

In Ireland you can hardly notice that it is raining if you were indoors, because you won't hear any noises on the roof of your house. I became scared at some point as I remember suddenly the Bible story of Noah and his ark, and wondered if it was the same kind of rain that caused the flood.

It was very disturbing to me, but Becky was sleeping so deeply that she couldn't hear any of it until when she woke up to go to the bathroom. I didn't find the need to switch on the air conditioner in our room because the air in the room was very in some way cool and relaxing by the time that the rain subsided, and I slept like a baby afterwards.

In spite of the rain, the early morning brought strong sunshine and warmth. Becky woke up looking very tired as if she hadn't slept all night not withstanding the fact that she was fast asleep duration that torrential rain thunder, threatened to pull down the entire city. Uncle Bill also noticed Becky's dullness when we went to the restaurant to have our breakfast.

Even though he asked Becky what was wrong with her, she refused to tell him anything tangible, just murmuring, "I'm just very tired" Uncle Bill decided that she might be suffering from a simple headache and offered her some paracetamol tablets.

Nonetheless, we set out quite early after eating breakfast, but we still got caught up in the morning traffic. Uncle Bill said it was due to the heavy downpour in the night.

"You don't look too well, what's the matter?" I asked Becky, as we got in the cab.

"Nothing really," replied Becky. "It's just that…"

"Just that what?" Uncle Bill asked Becky, interrupting from where he was sitting in the front passenger's seat.

"Eh, nothing papa, I'm fine," Becky answered. "I'm 'red' right now," Becky whispered into my ear shortly.

"You're red, what do you mean you're red?" I asked gently, not understanding her turn of phrase at all.

"Aren't you a girl? You're supposed to understand what I'm talking about, Sandra," she said.

"Sorry, but I don't read minds," I replied. "Maybe you should explain what you really mean,"

"What are you two going on about?" asked Uncle Bill.

"It's nothing, we're just chatting," I replied sharply to Uncle Bill.

"I see," Uncle Bill simply said and then turned carried on chatting to the driver of the taxi.

"I'm having my period, you know!" Becky said to me slowly.

"Mm, I get your point now, and I suppose that you've taken charge of the situation proper, if you know what I mean," I told her kindly, and she in turn nodded positively.

"That's why I'm not very cheerful this morning, I feel very weak and I hate it," she said.

"Try to take it off your mind and cheer up, we're going to have a good time today," I said warmly.

"You can imagine on a fun day out like this, I'm never going to feel free, and I'm very upset with myself right now," Becky said regretfully.

"Actually, there's no need to feel that way, it's not the end of the world, and I told her. I can imagine how you're feeling, but just try to ignore it. My mum said she had it on her wedding day," I told her.

"That was most unfortunate, if that happens to me I'll perceive it as a curse," she replied.

The two of us, I mean Becky kept on murmuring and whispering to ourselves, and Uncle Bill was getting suspicious, "Is everything alright there?" he asked yet again. And we gave him just the answers that anyone in that shoe would give. "We're fine here Uncle Bill, don't worry about us, everything is just great," I replied. But underneath I knew that it was a blatant white lie, because when you find yourself hiding something, then you should know that something is very wrong, but unfortunately you don't tell this type of problem to a *dad*, I don't know why, but maybe mums are the expert in that sort of thing.

Mum said to me once that the *red stuff* was an entirely a girl's affair and I don't like to talk to my dad about it too. I remembered one particular day that I was feeling under the weather for the same reason, and my dad, you know as a doctor, he started to ask me questions. And just when I was about to blab out the reason behind my funny mood, mum appeared hurriedly from the kitchen, signalling me not to say anything to my dad.

It was more than two hours before we got past the terrible hold-up. By then Uncle Bill was getting very impatient with the taxi driver, as if it was his fault.

"What do you want me to do, fly?" the driver had repeatedly said to Uncle Bill, as Uncle Bill, himself, did not stop to put pressure on him. He continually said to the driver that he was getting too late for his meeting. And he'd wanted the driver to go faster despite the bad traffic, maybe fly really, if that was only possible.

I heaved a sigh of relief when the driver drove into the enormous compound of the government secretariat buildings and finally stopped the car. Then we walked into this gigantic building, it was all painted white, and the reception hall was well decorated with beautiful cushioned chairs, with artificial flowers carefully placed in every corner of the walls.

Becky and I waited in the reception area while Uncle Bill went into one of the offices to attend his meeting. Later, when he came out, the three of us walked to the roadside to get another taxi that would take us to the bank where Uncle Bill was going to collect the money that my dad had sent to him through wire transfer.

There was a long queue inside the Banking Hall when we got there, and I was quite impressed to see people queuing up for a change. When it got to the turn of the man in front of Uncle Bill, trouble ensued all of a sudden between the man and the cashier, thereby causing long delays for the rest of the people in the queue. The man protested that he wouldn't leave the queue or the banking hall for that matter, without his money. While the cashier threatened to call security, he did not relent one bit.

"All I want is my money, please pay me my money," the customer yelled repeatedly.

"Gentleman, why are you being so difficult? You've withdrawn every single kobo (cent) and you've got nothing remaining in your account," the cashier explained to him gently.

"I think you people are trying to steal my money, you think that I'm that forgetful. The last time I came here to withdraw some cash from my account, I knew that I still had one hundred naira left in my account," the customer replied accusingly.

"Stop embarrassing yourself, young man. Your account is empty and if you don't leave right now, I'm calling security," the cashier threatened.

"Call security if you like. I'm not leaving without my money. Please pay me my money, please pay my money, please pay my money," the customer pleaded over and over as the other customers looked at him pathetically.

The cashier picked up the phone from his table and dialled a number, before long two police-uniformed men walked into the banking hall, and headed towards the cashier's table. I knew that they had come to take the difficult customer away. I moved swiftly close to the customer and asked him to tell me exactly how much that he wanted to withdraw from his account. His replied that he had, one hundred naira still remaining inside his account, and that was all he had left in this entire world.

I quickly reached into my handbag and there was some money left inside, a lot more than what the man was hassling for, and I brought out exactly one hundred naira and gave to him, to the glare of all the other customers as they watched in amazement.

"Thank you very much, and may the good Lord bless you and your family," said the customer gratefully, as he took the money from me and then walked out of the banking hall.

"What did you do that for?" Uncle Bill asked snappily.

"Because I feel pity for him," I replied softly.

"You're always having pity for everybody. Is it how you're going to keep sharing money to anyone you meet outside? Let me tell you something, you certainly can't become fairy godmother to all these people. There're too many in dare need of financial help in this city, and you can't carry on sharing your money in this manner," Uncle Bill said grudgingly.

Well, Uncle Bill carried on grumbling for a while longer, he told me that if I had so much money to share, that I should better hold on as there are a lot more people in the village who needed the money more desperately than the strangers that I met on the streets of Lagos city.

I told him that I didn't quite agree with him because it was only a small token, but more importantly, it was from my heart.

There was a woman that was standing next to me, she said that she recognised the difficult customer as one of the people who regularly scavenges for empty cans and bottles in the big refuse dump centre near her home.

I am devastated about seeing little children hawking in the streets, and about Becky's sad story. And now it's about grown up people scavenging from garbage bins in order to make a living, it's so unbelievable, and I don't understand why no one seems to care about the welfare of these poor people.

I kept thinking about it while walking with Becky and her dad to the main road to catch another cab.

Becky still found it difficult to get in a good in the midst of everything that was going on. She must have been feeling very uneasy with that *red* stuff, you know?

Not long after we left the bank, Becky started to complain that she had something to collect from her mom's place, Uncle Bill didn't want anything to disturb us further, he just wanted the driver to drive us straight to the beach, but Becky persisted, and in the end he agreed that we should all go to Becky's house together first before the beach.

Uncle Bill directed the driver to reverse and take us to somewhere in Kirikiri-Town, certainly not one of those posh places that Becky counted, but uncle told me that Kirikiri-Town was famous in some other way. That was where they have a very mighty prison; the Kirikiri-Maximum prison where they dump all criminals from Lagos state, Uncle Bill even mentioned that he'd once witnessed a shooting of some armed bandits when he went the town to pass on a message to a friend from his own village who lived close to the prison itself.

We narrowly missed Becky's step dad by the time that we got to their house; her mom told us that he left home only a few minutes earlier. However, I noticed that Uncle Bill and Becky's mom behaved in such a harmonious way with each other, they still got on so well just like very good friends, their divorce withstanding. Unlike one of my friend's parents, they'd been separated for a very long time, but still argued with each other anytime they happened to meet. And that happened quite a lot of times because my friend stays with both of them, though one at time and the other parent has to drop her off, you know, and that made them come in contact with each other quite often. *Shame!*

"Your mother must be a white woman," Becky's mom said with a smile when she saw me.

"Yes," I replied politely.

"You must be blind to ask that question in the first place, isn't it too obvious that her mum is white, and by the way, have you forgotten I told you sometime ago that my brother was getting married to a white girl in the republic of Ireland?" asked Uncle Bill teasingly.

"Yeah, I remember now, but it was a long time ago. I'm bound to forget you know," replied Becky's mum.

"But Sandra isn't white," Becky said wittily.

"So what do you call her then, black?" her mum asked funnily.

"She is white and black mixed together, and that is known as a mulatto. She is a mulatto, yea Sandra, isn't that the word?" Becky said, looking very uncertain about her explanation.

"Yeah," I nodded.

"A mulatto?" Uncle Bill asked timidly.

"Papa," Becky called. "I'm sure you haven't heard of that word before, have you? I just wonder if you people ever used the dictionary in the olden days."

"Becky's behaviour has changed very badly in the last year. I think that this city's crazy lifestyle is affecting her. And I hope that she hasn't been following in a group of bad girls in her school," Uncle Bill complained bitterly about Becky to her mum.

"No. First of all, Becky is a good girl, and second of all, her school is one of the strictest ones around here, and lastly, she was only joking, weren't you Becky?" her mom said, defensively.

"Um, Sure," Becky replied cleverly.

"Now apologise to your father," urged her mom.

"Papa doesn't know how to take a simple joke. She said. I mean I'm sorry, Papa, it won't happen again," Becky said finally.

"Excuse my forgetfulness, Sandra. Let me offer you something to eat. I've some akara (bean-cakes) in the kitchen," Becky's mum said to me nicely.

No, thanks, I'm very full at the moment," I replied.

"What a shame! Maybe when you come around next time," she said.

"Yeah, next time," I responded sharply.

Nevertheless, Becky's mom seemed like a very humble and pleasant person, and she offered to give me some palm oil to give to my dad in Dublin if I could stop by on my way from the village. Becky didn't really take anything from her mum's house, I'm sure she only wanted me to see her mum.

The sun was beginning to set by the time we got to the beach; nonetheless, the weather looked bright and lovely, except that it was still too hot for me. There were an awful lot of people out on the beach, just walking up and down by the shores. Some others rode on horses, while some kids busied themselves selling things as usual. No one was actually swimming in the sea, which looked ferocious with the mighty waves coming and going from the shore.

Uncle Bill forbade Becky and I to go close to the waves, claiming that many people had gone missing from the beach before. But Becky said that her dad didn't live in Lagos city and probably doesn't know what he was talking about, as she, her mum and step dad had been to the beach on several occasions and never heard about any such incidents before. Anyway, we had some fun riding on horses back later on, until my brain started sensing something good cooking in the air.

The delicious aroma of roasted kebabs filled everywhere, I couldn't resist the temptations not to have some as I watched the men preparing and then serve their customers. Uncle Bill later bought some, which was served with red-hot chill and onion rings. If the soft drinks vendors were to be so far away from us, I would have fainted, as I nearly choked on the hot chilli. I really haven't eaten anything so hot in my entire life before. And it was my fault entirely, because I tried to imitate Becky who chewed on raw —hot—chilli peppers. But I felt as though my chest was burning so hot and I had to guzzle down many sips from the bottle in a hurry to help cool the burning sensation in my chest.

After the chilli—madness was over, I bought some banana ice creams and sat down quietly under the raffia tent and watched the waves come and go. Then soon after, some local drummers came around to entertain us for a small tip. First, they demanded to know my name, and when I told them, they quickly composed a beautiful song using my name. It sounded so wonderful as they sang something like; *Sandra, omor—owoh* many times, with the group leader starting first, and the rest of the group went like *Omor—owo, Omor—Owoooooo!!*

And with the Yoruba traditional beating of the drums, I reckon any good music producer would have been tempted to sign them on, on the sport. 'Ha —ha—ha.'

Later, Uncle Bill interpreted the meaning of the song to me; he said that it was a praise singing song in Yoruba language, the song referred to me as a *rich* girl. I wish I was, but the truth is that I wasn't rich at all, except that I was far better off than most of them. Uncle Bill didn't speak Yoruba, but he said that it was quite easy; anyone can tell the meanings to the song. He even joked that if only I'd listened more carefully, that I would have understood the meanings by myself.

Shortly after, Becky and I found the perfect excuse to have a little stroll down to the shoreline to pick some seashells and pebbles. But it wasn't long before Uncle Bill called us back, because we had to get back to the hotel soon, to enable us check out and then go to the bus station on time in order to secure our seats in the luxury coach that was billed to take us to the village.

"I can't wait to get to the village," I said.

"Not too long now. By this time tomorrow we'll have arrived in the village," said Uncle Bill hopefully.

"I hope you can stand the pressure," Becky said.

"What are you talking about, pressure from what?" asked Uncle Bill, startled.

"I'm only pointing out that, there's every possibility that when we arrive in the in the village, all the little kids will want to come and see her," said Becky to her dad.

"Yes, hopefully that's not going to cause so much trouble for her and, besides, there's no way that we'll allow anyone to hassle her," Uncle Bill said to Becky.

"I know, but you remember how those kids like to run around any new visitor to the village," Becky pointed out.

"Noooooooooo," I screamed unexpectedly.

"What do you scream like that for?" asked Uncle Bill, surprised.

"Nothing, I must have bit my tongue by mistake," I lied.

Isn't that exactly what my mum and me talked about in the car, when she drove me to Dublin Airport to catch my first flight to London? I'm definitely in for another nightmare, and I'm not going to like it, I thought silently.

113

CHAPTER TEN
Mister B!

We arrived at the bus-terminus so late that we almost missed the next couch that was due to leave soon. And the place was overcrowded with long buses lined in rows, each one looking out for potential passengers travelling to various parts of the country. The bus terminus was the perfect description of the typical Lagos markets that I never saw, there were men, women and children trading all different kinds of things that you can imagine sellable under the sun. Even though it was night already, the traders still sold stuff; from fresh peppers and tomatoes, or fresh fish, fruits and vegetables to cooked foods, from fashions of different types and styles to electronics and electrical products, and many other things. I just wondered if the people in Lagos city remembered to go to sleep at night. I guess it was almost a matter of the *city that never sleeps*, just like New York City in the United States.

We successfully secured three seats for ourselves inside the bus, and soon two men smartly dressed in soldier uniforms soon came inside the bus, each holding a gun, they didn't look like the regular travellers in anyway, as they glanced swiftly at all the passengers as if they were out looking for a crime suspect inside the bus.

The two men did not get down from the bus and neither were they in any hurry to sit down, they paced from one end of the bus to the other until the driver was ready to move the vehicle, before they finally sat down. I felt a little intimidated by them, especially with those guns in their hands. It's not that I had not come in contact with a military personal with a gun before but being so close to those two guys made me very apprehensive. I felt as though they were going to get up from their seats any minute and start firing shots at everyone, and perhaps in the case of a hostage, I was going to be singled out as the only *white girl* in the couch. Anyway, it wasn't as if any of those things that I was busy imagining was going to happen, I was being cynical for no real reason. I suppose if there were a contest anywhere in the world to find the one person who has the most worrying mind, I'd be the winner.

And come to think of it, its kind of cool you know! When in Ireland, I'm mostly called a black girl, and as far as Africa was concerned, I'm a white girl—hurray!

"What are you worried about, Sandra, my daughter?" he asked. Uncle Bill must have figured out from the expression on my face that I was having some kind of worries.

"I'm not sure, Uncle Bill," I replied distractedly.

"But you are worried about something," Uncle Bill said. "It appears that you're feeling home sick already."

"No Uncle, Bill, it's not that at all," I said. "I think that I'm a bit worried about those two soldiers."

"You mean those two, you shouldn't have any silly suspicions about them," he said. "They're especially assigned for the purpose of the journey; to protect us from highway armed robbers who sometimes are in frequent operations between the routes."

My fears grew even worse when Uncle Bill said that, because my mind started to go wild about all the horrible things that could happen to someone merely on a journey.

I was somehow worried about air disaster while in the plane, and now I had to worry about an armed robbery attack. I'm just sick and tired of all the rubbish, I thought.

Nonetheless, the bus travelled smoothly throughout the night; with the driver stopping only once near a small village and asked that if any passenger wished to ease their self, so he could to get down to do so. We got to another big city soon after that. It was more or less like in Lagos city, and I mean hawking between vehicles. Uncle Bill told me that it was called Benin City.

It reminded me about a certain story, which my dad once told me about the old Benin Empire and the Benin Kingdom. It was quite amazing to see the very place that my dad had told me so much about.

Well, no one really came down there, as the driver had no cause to stop. We were just passing through the city. It was all like one big jolly ride, and by morning time, we had arrived safely in the big town nearest to Dad's village.

From where the bus had stopped at the waterfront, I could see Dad's village across the vast open sea.

"That's our village over there, we're going to be there very soon," said Uncle Bill. "And you're going to see your grandparents soon, okay?"

It was almost unbelievable. I kept smiling to myself until Becky suddenly brought me back to myself when she asked me what I was thinking. I simply had this beautiful feeling inside me and I didn't know what to call it. The feeling was simply too incredible to describe.

The flowing river looked so wide and it began to scare me as I stared at the big waves being caused by all different types of boats; decked dingy-boats, small canoes and speedboats all loading and off-loading passengers from the harbour. Everything and everywhere seemed so strange, though. I felt like I was in a movie in my dreams or something, especially as people gazed steadily at me as though I was some kind of a super star from the city or out of space perhaps.

In the riverbank, children and adults alike bathed in the water. They swam and splashed. Most of the kids were completely naked and didn't care if anyone was looking at them, and they showed an utterly carefree attitude as they jumped in and out of the water. I found myself completely lost as I watched them. It seemed like a totally new world to me and I just wondered why I had not made the decision to visit earlier.

I mean this is my country too, and I know absolute nothing about it, except the little that my dad has told me. Experience is the best teacher they say. Now I've come and I'm definitely going to learn a lot, I thought as I brought out my camera to take pictures of those bathing in the water. None of them made any attempt to complain, they just smiled at the camera. It was such a beautiful thing.

Becky later explained to me that most of the local people didn't have bathrooms in their homes so it was either they fetched water from the sea and used it to take their bath openly in their backyard, or simply went to the river to splash. And the majority preferred going to splash out in the big sea.

"We shall go in that one," Uncle Bill said, pointing to a white and blue coloured speedboat. The driver or the controller kept on yelling "Ogu-Apapa, Ogu-Apapa."

I felt completely alarmed just looking into the water, and my mind resumed once more, imagining myself falling into the big sea and struggling to swim out, but I couldn't because the tide's been so strong, it kept pushing further and further into the middle of the river, until I was swept away eventually.

"You look horrible. Is everything okay with you?" Becky asked suddenly, bringing me back from a dim-witted trance.

"Everything is fine, but what can we do in case the boat overturns in the middle of the sea?" I asked anxiously.

"Ha, ha, ha!" Becky laughed out loud. "So you're petrified of the big sea?" she asked sarcastically. I hope that nothing terrible happens to us."

"Listen to me, Becky, I love my mom and dad very much and I don't want anything dreadful happening to me that might cause me not see them ever again," I said to Becky seriously.

Don't worry nothing bad will happen to you and, besides, if something does happen, I'll help you," Becky teased.

"What? I can't swim well in a big sea like this, I only know how to swim in the swimming pool. I can't risk my life to cross this big sea, I might as well go back home from here, because my mind isn't that strong to face this type of danger," I said.

"Hey! You're taking this too seriously. Nothing is going to happen to us just because we're going to be crossing the sea."

"Everybody here including students travel to and from, in a boat, in case you haven't noticed that it's the only form of transport in this area," she replied.

"Are you sure we're going to be safe?" I asked anxiously.

"You don't expect that we swim across the sea, do you? And moreover these boats are very dependable, and by the way, what I said earlier about something terrible happening was only meant to be a joke," Becky said ruefully.

"Thanks, it's not that I'm too scared anyway. After all, Ireland is a country that is surrounded by water, it's just that the situation here is a little bit different because I've never ever been inside one of these types of boats before," I told Becky.

I was grateful that Uncle Bill wasn't a complete illiterate, because only Becky wouldn't have been able to interpret everything to me. I was made to understand later that the same town where the coach dropped us was the central focus in the community. Because it was the only town around which had motor park, and also where you could find a post office, police station, secondary schools, a general hospital, open market place and other important governmental agencies, though small, it was quite a busy township, which attracted traders, students and low-income workers similarly from the neighbouring villages.

"It's time, girls, let's get in the boat," Uncle Bill shouted over.

"But I thought that the 'Day Spring' hotel where we stayed in Lagos was located in the Apapa vicinity. How come the boat driver is yelling the same?" I asked unwittingly." I hope he won't be taking us going back to Lagos from the sea." If you don't know something, then you have to ask questions, unless you choose to remain naïve about it forever. Agree that I still had tons of different things to learn about my new environment, but I could still remember that the hotel that we stayed in Lagos was located at Apapa. If only for the Apapa Amusemnt Park, I didn't have to forget that name so soon. And I thought that it was obvious there has to be some type of explanations to why a particular boat driver was calling for passengers that were going to Apapa if not the same one in side the big city of Lagos. But because I asked, Uncle Bill had plenty also to tell me about it, which I found the following explanations interesting too, because my dad hadn't told me about it before.

"No, Sandra, our village, Ogu, is divided in two different zones. The mainland is Ogu and the second part is known as Apapa," explained Uncle Bill sweetly.

"How come my dad never told me about like this before?" I asked Uncle Bill probingly.

"Your father's mind is not a computer. I don't blame him for not remembering to tell you everything about our village, after all it' been such a long time since he left the village," said Uncle Bill defensively.

Becky got into the boat smartly. I only did with the help of Uncle Bill; he virtually carried me inside the boat, as it was quite steep to get in from the jetty on the harbour. I noticed that all the other passengers starred at me strangely, probably wondering what 'a white girl' was looking for in that remote part of the country. We were on our way soon as the boat zoomed out into the vast ocean, which was the final part of my adventurous journey to dad's village. I sat clinging unto Becky like a crying baby would to his mum because I'd been terrified at the speed that the boat was moving on the waters. It seemed to my eyes as if it was doing a million miles per second.

"Hey, Mister B!" I heard someone called to Uncle Bill. Where have you been all this while? Your wife said that you travelled to Lagos city, I guess you've been up to one of those pension-chasing trips of yours again, haven't you?" asked a skinny looking man with bushy hair, from one of the seats in the front of the boat.

I wondered why he and Uncle Bill did not notice each other on the harbour before getting on the boat, if they knew themselves that well.

"Ah! It's you, Mr. Okoro. Where are you coming from this early morning?" asked Uncle Bill.

"When I said that baby girls brought good luck to the family, no one ever believes me. I hope you still remember my younger sister, Benita, who got married two years ago to that famous builder in the other village next to the long bridge. Well, she's just given birth to a beautiful baby girl," the strange looking man said to Uncle Bill.

"Congratulations! When did she have the baby?" Uncle Bill said happily.

"Only yesterday, and I've been over to see them since then," the man replied with a broad smile.

"How are the new mother and the baby doing?" Uncle Bill asked.

"Great, they're doing just fine. The baby looks so much like my own mother, but sadly, my in-law argued that she resembled his mother, which is untrue."

"And I must tell you that if your wife gives birth to a baby girl, be happy, be very happy," said the man.

"Why?" Uncle Bill asked him intently.

"Do you want to know why?" he asked Uncle Bill. "First of all, my sister gave birth to a baby girl, and next thing her husband gets a contract. Can you believe that my sister's husband received a letter only this morning, informing him that he'd been awarded the contract to build a new administrative block in their local school compound, the same contract that he'd been struggling to get for years. So how else do you explain that?" he said.

"I don't know. Why don't you explain to me," replied Uncle Bill.

"Isn't it obvious that it was because his wife gave birth to a baby girl?" he queried.

"Yeah, which is good news, but I still don't see the connection between the fact that your sister's new baby brought luck to the father and the way that you're making it sound like."

"I'm sure that your brother in-law would still have received the same news if your sister's baby was a boy. And furthermore, all new babies are believed equally to bring good luck to their parents, whether baby boy or baby girl," Uncle Bill said to him while I listened with rapt attention.

Soon the boat stopped at the Apapa waterside and some of the passengers disembarked, including the strange Mr.Okoro.

"Bye, I'll come over to your house later in the evening," Mr. Okoro said to Uncle Bill as he waved goodbye to him.

"Alright, see you later," replied Uncle Bill.

"Who was that funny man?" I asked Becky, curiously.

"Do you mean Mr. Okoro? He teaches in the village primary school," Becky replied promptly.

"He's a teacher?" I asked, surprisingly.

"He was transferred from one of the eastern states to come and teach in our village, and he doesn't understand a word of our native dialect," Becky explained.

"Was it so much trouble for him and the pupils not understanding each other?" I asked Becky.

"Well, as you have seen, his only form of communication is English, which a majority of the people in the village including the pupils don't understand very well. But the most annoying thing about Mr. Okoro is that he drinks alcohol like fishes drink water in the sea," Becky told me.

"Um, some teacher that he is," I said quietly.

"You can say that again. Once Mr. Okoro got so drunk that he mistook a papaya tree for his enemy. He began punching the tree until someone saw him and tried to stop him. The next day, his pupils got wind of the news and they teased and jeered at him in school," Becky told me.

"I wonder if the children still have any respect left for him," I said.

"Respect indeed, what kind of respect does he deserve by the pupils when he hasn't got any for himself. They only fear him because he's a bully."

"He whips them so hard with his koboko-cane for every silly excuse," Becky said.

"I don't believe this," I said.

"Better believe this one. Mr. Okoro really gives each child up to ten lashes of the cane if they're late and calls it *Morning Tea*. He's very notorious for that," Becky said.

"So why do the villagers tolerate him then?" I asked. "Why don't they report him to the educational board?"

"Last year some parents went to complain to the village chief to have him replaced because of his drunken behaviours; however, that didn't happen. That's why he is still around," Becky answered.

"So he is one hell of a drunkard. No wonder he spoke like one," I said to Becky.

Finally the boat got to the main Ogu-village waterside and berthed, then all the remaining passengers got off, as new ones who'd been waiting rushed inside.

CHAPTER ELEVEN
Here We Are!

"Here we are! Welcome to your father's homeland," Uncle Bill said to me.

I stood speechless for a while, just looking around at the beautiful green vegetation that surrounded me. There was a huge sugarcane plantation just by the other side of the shore nearer to the Apapa riverside, it was so vast that that you couldn't really see to where it ended. Then looking directly across the sea was what seemed like a beautiful beach, no one was really there, other than women paddling in their canoes. There was a huge green land just by the other side of the shore, which appeared to be another sugarcane plantation. It was so vast that it was the only thing that you couldn't really see from where it started or ended. Then from directly across the sea was what seemed like a beautiful beach, the pure white sand appeared almost glittery everywhere. I couldn't believe it, that I was actually standing on the same soil where my dad had been born and grew up; something I'd only thought about in my imagination not so long ago. It didn't quite sink in that it was real, and not one of my wildest thinking that was starting to torment me again.

I quickly reached for my camera and took photos of the tall coconut and palm trees, which lined the riverbank on end. Everywhere was calm, not completely quiet, though, as there were the sounds of paddles going in and out of water, and that of passing engine boats and tiny whispers of flying birds up in the sky. Nevertheless, it was still very quiet and silent in a very special way to me. I felt so peaceful inside.

"Snap out of it," I said to myself softly, as Uncle Bill soon prompted that we start walking.

"Once again, you're welcomed," Uncle Bill said happily to me one more time.

"Sure, Uncle Bill, thanks," I replied excitedly.

I tried pushing my trolley-bag, but that wasn't easy as the road was unpaved. Becky didn't waste much time in lifting the heavily loaded bag on top of her head. We walked quite a long distance between the waterside and the main town. There were small farms on both sides of the road leading to the village itself, and I saw some people ploughing, planting seeds of various crops. I just wondered why people were on their farms so early in the morning.

As we walked through what seemed like the high street, I saw children dressed in their school uniforms. They had their school bags, which in some cases were ordinary carrier bags, in their hands or on their heads just as Becky had carried my baggage. They were all heading to school with bare foot, except for a very few that wore flip-flops. They appeared very happy and content, not caring about anything else in the world. As soon as they saw me, they started whispering something to each other. Some of them soon recognised Becky and began calling out her name, she could only wave to them because of the heavy bag on her head.

"I couldn't carry such a heavy bag on my head, I guess I'd just slump and fall instantly if I tried," I whispered quietly to Becky. She smiled and said that children in the village who were much younger than her were able to carry even bigger loads, like a basket-full of cassava or cocoa-yam on their heads and walk a long distance from their mothers' farms back to the village without much difficulty.

"Wow!" was all that I could mutter, not because I doubted her, but it simply sounded unbelievable to me.

I was eager to get to Uncle Bill's house, so I can finally meet my grandparents, hug them, and just sit next to them and feel their warmth. I wouldn't mind if they might be too old and weak to lift me, but I could cuddle up to them if I wanted, just like I did with my maternal grandma in Ireland.

There were all different kinds of houses that I saw on the way; some mud houses with carefully thatched roofs, and some others that were roofed with sheets of zinc, and then there were some blockhouses as well. While some were simply wrapped over with huge waterproof bags just like garden sheds. I was so shocked to notice that some women cooked in the open air with dry firewood.

As we went along, I wondered what Uncle Bill's house looked like. I wondered if it would turn out to be just like one of the waterproof wrap around ones. I also wondered how the inhabitants in those types of houses managed during serious winds and torrential rains. Well, the truth was about to be revealed. Surprisingly, we soon walked into a lovely compound that was surrounded by beautiful plants and flowers. There was a cute story building in the middle of the yard, which I presumed must be where the Chief lived. Because if compared to all the other types of houses that I saw, it would be like the proverbial saying about the 'one eyed king in the city of the blinds'. But it turned out it wasn't the Chief's palace at all, however what Uncle Bill told me about the pretty house was not expected, I was shocked rather.

"This is where I live, but it is, in fact, your father's house," Uncle Bill told me.

"What do you mean, this is my father's house? That's not possible, my dad never mentioned that he had a house in Africa," I said, startled.

That was not possible. I thought that it was not possible in the first place that my dad owned the house, because my dad hadn't talked about him having any other house anywhere besides the one in Dublin. And there was no way that Uncle Bill could be right. But if it turned out that the house belonged to my dad really, then I just might be in for a surprise of a lifetime, most likely to find out many more secrets about my dad.

I also suddenly found myself praying silently that I wasn't going to discover a step-sister or brother somewhere along the line, because I've heard some rumours before that my dad had another child. Actually I only overheard Mum and Dad arguing about it a long time ago, I later discovered that Mum also found out from elsewhere that Dad had the child in Nigeria before he travelled to Ireland where he met my mum. Dad branded the story as complete rubbish. He said that it was simply part of the devil's plan to try to destroy his happy marriage. Though I did not hear anymore of it except Mum saying she believed Dad completely. She put it like this, "Your dad and I are going to stick together and fight the devil into submission."

I had no clue to the meaning of that statement and never bothered to worry about it afterwards; however, Uncle Bill seemed stunned too that my dad hadn't mentioned the house to Mum and me.

"Are you very sure that your father had never mentioned to you and your mother that he's a proud owner of this lovely house?" asked Uncle Bill, confused.

"No," I answered.

"But why not?" he queried.

Uncle Bill, are you going to show me to my dad's child in the village?" I asked unexpectedly.

"What, did your dad say that he had a child in the village? This is surely surprising to me, because I have no idea about the existence of such a child," he said.

"Are you sure, Uncle Bill?" I asked.

"Yes, I'm sure," he said and then paused for a short while. "I'm just wondering why your father kept such a secret from me. Before he left, I used to think that we knew everything about each other."

"Well...maybe not," I replied defensively. "But I was wondering that if Dad could keep a secret about this house from Mum and me then what else wasn't possible?"

"D-do you mean that your father actually told you and your mother that he has another child?" asked Uncle Bill almost eagerly.

"No, I was only being investigative for my Mum's sake, seriously," I replied.

"But why, or did you ever hear the two of them in an argument about soothing like this before?" he questioned.

"To be honest, yes, they have. And Dad denied it," I said.

"Um, sounds like some over-jealous friends had been on the prowl, anyway let's leave it for now, but rest assured that your father does not have another child here."

"I hope not," I said quietly.

"And you know something about the question of this house? I think that your father is keeping it a secret from you and your mother, so that it will be a big surprise when he decides that you all come back and live here permanently."

"No, Uncle Bill, I don't think that Dad will ever want us to move here finally, unless on holidays. Besides Mum would not let him do that," I told Uncle Bill.

"Your mother, does she always tell him what to do?" he asked, upset.

"Sometimes," I replied.

"That is not very customary. In African culture, only the man decides what should and should not be done in the family," said Uncle Bill crossly.

"What makes you think that what you've said is the normal one, Uncle Bill? In fact, why should the man be the only person to make decisions in a home?" I asked him bluntly.

"You'll understand why when you're much older, he said, after taking a deep breath."

"Anyway, as I was saying, your father sent the money for me to take care of all the building expenditures from the beginning right to the completion of the house," explained Uncle Bill.

"Um, I see," I said nonchalantly.

"Your father grew up here, right in this very spot where this building is standing. And he..."

"Hey!" I said, interrupting. "I thought you mentioned only a while ago that my dad had sent the money for this house to be built, so how come he grew up in it?" I asked curiously.

"Don't get confused, Sandra. What I'm trying to tell you is that, before this house was built, there was another building right where this one is, and it was our parents' house—your grandparent's."

"It was an old mud house with thatched roof that leaked a lot whenever it rained. Our mother used to line the rooms with empty cups and buckets to catch the rain water, so..."

"That sounds very funny, Uncle Bill," I said interruptedly one more time.

"Um, you can say that now, but it used to be very bad at that time, especially if it rained so late at night, but because there wouldn't be enough dry space to lay our mats, and so we'd all be squashed together in the same sport," Uncle Bill said sadly.

"So what happened next?" I demanded.

"The house became so weak, all the blocks of mud started to give way. The once very strong woods inside had begun to rot as well, so my parents decided that it was better demolished for the safety of everyone who lived there, he explained. But that not withstanding, we all grew up in that crooked house, if you prefer to call it that."

I wondered why my dad failed to tell me all about the historic stories surrounding his upbringing, such as this one.

"Anyway, like I said," continued Uncle Bill. "After the demolition, the area had been vacant until two years ago when your father instructed and sent all the monies to have this magnificent story building erected to preserve our family name and respect," Uncle Bill explained, pleased.

"Where did grandma and grandpa live after the house was demolished?" I asked.

"I too used to be the proud owner of one small house at the time that the old house was demolished, and all of us managed to live there, although it's now being used as a barn to store fresh crops during the rainy season," he explained further.

Knock-knock. Uncle Bill knocked hard on the front gate, and immediately a fat lady, neatly dressed in native attire, came out running to open the gate.

Who is this person with such scattered hair and so many bangles dangling on her wrist like an Egyptian dancer? I wondered silently. Her head scarf had fallen off as she was hurrying to open the gate for the three of us.

Well, it turned out that she was Uncle Bill's second wife— Becky's step-mum.

The moment she opened the gate and saw us, she came forward to embrace Uncle Bill as she greeted him, and then Becky, and lastly me, after exchanging some words with Uncle Bill probably enquiring about who I was, after all she really wasn't expecting me.

Then she turned and hugged me and began to call out to everyone, possibly announcing our homecoming and soon the entire compound was full with people, but while inside the sitting room everyone turned their focus on me, which was quite expected.

Both adults and children alike, some in their school uniforms all came to greet me or rather to have a good look at me as if I was some alien that had only landed from space. I was astounded how so many people would turn out just to welcome someone. That aspect of people starring at me was quite embarrassing, but I felt very flattered all the same.

That morning, I met my paternal grandparents for the very first time—the feelings I couldn't express, but it was an unforgettable moment. Both of them had grown so old, though still looked physically strong in spite of the fact that their hair had all turned grey but even in that, I saw that they'd been very beautiful and handsome in their younger years.

Dad told me often that I reminded him of his mum. He'd been right all the time. And Uncle Bill repeated it when he first saw me at the airport in Lagos. He was right also; I had a remarkable resemblance to my grandma really. However, I genuinely thought that my dad was caught in the middle; he looked like his mum and dad altogether, because he had the same shape of face as his mum, and he had the same gap in between his front teeth just like his dad. Whenever my granddad smiled, even though weakly, it made me to think about how much I miss my dad because I almost could visualise my dad's face in his smiles.

The living room was jam-packed with people and air was tense as everyone took their turns in hugging me with the greetings of "Nuao, Wor-ya" meaning *welcome and how are you*.

Grandma insisted that I sat on her lap and Granddad couldn't stop smiling. It was clear that they were overjoyed about my visit. Uncle Bill became my interpreter as he patiently introduced everyone to me by his or her name and connection with the family. Beginning with all my aunts and uncles, nephews and nieces, cousins, and then the rest of them. It appeared to me like everybody in the entire village was inter-related one way or the other just like my dad used to tell me. The introductions went from one generation to the other. I remember a certain woman and Uncle Bill said that her great-grandfather was married to his sister-in-law's grandmother or something like that.

I became so, so fed up with the unending welcoming game, but I tried to be extra patient and polite so as not to get into anybody's bad record already. I so much wanted to please my grandparents and to make them feel proud of me, and the only way to do that was to be polite with everybody.

There was a general feeling of excitement everywhere in the compound and possibly the entire village. I'd been so happy as more and more people came in to welcome me. Tears started to roll down from my eyes as I thought about the merriment-taking place just for my sake. But then I noticed that the room had gone silent all of a sudden and everyone began to stare at me. It was the look of worry.

Uncle Bill then asked why I was crying. Seeing the tears on my face must have shocked them all to think that something had suddenly gone wrong with me. I had learned so much already about my dad's people after only a few hours of my arrival. The people of my dad's village simply do not express joyful emotions with tears, as I was later made aware of.

"I'm not crying, Uncle Bill," I replied, wiping off the tears with a small handkerchief, which I bought in Lagos city.

"So why the tears then? All these people think that something is making you to cry," Uncle Bill said, worried.

"I'm not crying, Uncle. It's just that I'm overwhelmed with everything, that's all," I said, grinning.

As soon as he interpreted the reasons for my tears to the crowd, the whole room returned with cheers and clapping.

If not for Uncle Bill and Becky I'd have been lost, as I didn't understand a single word that they spoke. I'd been a little apprehensive, unnecessarily though, but I'd wished silently at one time that my dad was present so I'd be rest assured that everything was fine, it doesn't matter whether or not I understood what they said, and my uncle and my cousin were doing a great job interpreting.

Later a bowl of cola nuts and bottles of drinks began to appear on top of the small wooden table in the middle of the fairly wide living room. There were beer bottles, Coke, Sprite and Fanta bottles and then a big gallon of what looked like common water to me at first, but when it was poured out smelt like alcohol. It was their favourite drink, and little children were not allowed to touch it. It was meant only for the grown ups. Also, Uncle Bill said that the locals brewed it and they called it *Ogogoro*.

Before they shared the drinks Granddad stood up to make a special speech, but was interrupted by a young man who had brought another gallon of drink with him. As he stepped inside the room, everyone cheered, "Palmy, palmy," and I'd thought that the guy must be called Mr. Palmy.

The gentleman opened the gallon and began to pour out some drink into a big calabash. It was whitish, and I'd thought that it was coconut milk. It looked unusually watery, though, but so fresh and inviting. I wanted to taste it so badly.

"I love coconut milk, can I have some?" I asked Uncle Bill.

"It isn't coconut milk, this is fresh palm-wine and it taste nice.

"You can taste some of it if you want. There isn't alcohol in it, but too much of it might intoxicate," he told me clearly.

Yeah right! There's no alcohol in it, so how come too much can intoxicate if it was actually non-alcohol like juices, I thought to myself.

"As you all know, in our tradition prayers come first before anyone can start to drink, so I expect every one of you to be patient," Granddad said to the crowd.

First he stood up from his old wooden, extraordinary

looking chair, and then poured some of the ogogoro drink to the ground to invite the ancestors. Then Granddad carried on summoning and praying until one time that I heard him mention something about Jerusalem and everyone chorused, "Amen."

CHAPTER TWELVE
Home Cooking

I'd had a wonderful day and was feeling really tired. I decided to ask Uncle Bill to show me any room where I might be staying in the house.

He then asked Becky and I to follow him to one of the rooms in the house, which seemed to be cleaned and sprayed with air freshener not too long before. It smelt fresh and lovely. There was a double bed which had been laid out properly with soft floral cotton with matching pillowcases. Surprisingly, though, there was an en-suite bathroom. I wondered just how it was possible to see such luxury in such a remote village; however, there was no running water from the tap when I tried to fill up the bathtub to have a good soak later.

Uncle Bill later explained to me that the room was specially reserved for my parents whenever they would visit, as no other person had slept there before. I felt really honoured as he said that it would be my own room throughout my stay with them.

"Becky will be here to keep you company if you don't want to be by yourself, and don't forget that if you need anything, just anything at all, all you have to do is ask and she'll help you to get it," Uncle Bill told me before leaving the room.

Later Becky's step-mum brought in a big plastic container and filled it up with water for our use.

"This time you stay here with us I take care for you," Becky's step-mum said to me in a bastardised English accent. You can call me mama-Tessie if you like because if anything you want or if you hungry, no problem. You tell me, I give you because I look after you very well, okay?"

"Yes, and thank you" I replied politely.

"Okay, now I go to my kitchen and wait," she said finally, and walked out of the room.

"Wow!" I mumbled. Wondering whether I actually understood what the woman was telling me.

"What do you say that for?" Becky asked, surprised.

"That was quite dramatic," I said.

"I think you should be happy that she can relate to you in English at all, because not so many women in this village can speak English any better than my step-mum," Becky said, grinning.

"Fantastic. But I hope you know that the two of us are meant to be staying in this room together, because I can't imagine myself sleeping alone at night in here," I said to Becky.

"I suppose so, besides you should know that in this family at the moment, your needs come first and I'll like to say that your word is my command," said Becky receptively. "Although you've got nothing to worry about as I'll be with you at all times."

"What could I have done without you, you're such a good person," I said to Becky admiringly.

And I really meant what I said, because she'd been so superbly close to me, as if we'd known each other for so long, most especially, she trusted me to reveal her darkest secrets. I think it's as the old saying goes; *Blood is thicker than water*.

Tessie's mum (Becky's step-mum) meant it that she was going to wait for us in her kitchen, as I'd only began to dress up after I came out of the bath when I heard her calling out Becky's name.

Granddad and Grandma were already there in the kitchen with Tessie's mum by the time Becky and I got there.

There was a sweet and delicious smell that was coming from Mama-Tessie's cooking. It was almost irresistible. As we walked into the kitchen, which was a small hut outbuilding beside the main house itself, my tummy began to rumble like two big hippos fighting each other in a puddle.

"You are very, very hungry," Tessie's mum said assumingly. "Please sit down my 'pikin' (child)."

The dining area was a simple, plain wooden table, surrounded with four DIY-type chairs. I wasn't very sure about eating the food at first, as I thought about the possibility of food poisoning for the first time, which was because I hadn't eaten any food cooked by a *typical* village woman before. But when I tried the first spoonful, it tasted so good that I found myself savouring every tasty mouthful. It was a meal of plantain porridge cooked with bush meat.

Later that evening some children brought me some nice fruits, some of which I'd obviously not seen or tasted before, but there was a certain one that caught my fancy the most. It was green and looked like a mango; it also tasted like mango except that it was a different type of fruit.

When I'd finished eating one, Becky cut it open with a cutlass, and we found a brown in oval shaped stone inside, again she kind of broke the stone into two yet there was seed inside, brown on the outside and pure white inside.

I grabbed the seed from Becky and threw it inside my mouth, Becky tried to stop me from chewing it; however, I'd been too fast and my teeth had bit on a small part of it, and it was gooey inside my mouth.

I made of fool of myself and the little kids heartily at me, it formed some kind of entertainment for them. But frankly, I wasn't embarrassed at all; I was glad that I made them laugh.

I was told that those brown seeds that we found inside the fruit were not meant to be eaten raw, although the seeds were edible, but in a different way. It was the popular *ogbono* seeds and can only be eaten by way of blending them first, then used to prepare a certain African soup, which the Africans love to eat very much.

Grandma and Grandpa smiled as they watched me mess about with those fruits and the seeds. I was very pleased to see my paternal grandparents watching over me. It was what I'd always wanted since I was little, and I'll cherish that moment forever.

It was getting dark and everywhere started to light up with small kerosene lanterns. I began to worry about what I'd do without proper electricity to light up my room. I'd not slept in darkness before and I knew very well that the mosquitoes bit more in the night. So the only thing on my mind as the day became greyer and greyer was what I would do to keep them at bay. I was scared that the mosquitoes in the village might defy the effect of the repellents and make a feast of my skin in the night.

"I'm worried that I might end up in the emergency ward tomorrow morning," I whispered to myself.

All the shiny white ceiling fans hung in the ceilings of all the rooms, yet they couldn't function because of lack of electricity in the village.

"This is so bad," I blurted out without realising that I was talking.

"What do you mean?" Becky questioned.

"Never mind, it's nothing," I lied.

"You mentioned something being so bad. Was it the food?" asked Becky.

"No, how can you even think that? I really enjoyed eating my food, and besides, I emptied everything in my plate. I must let you know that Tessie's mum's a good cook," I replied to Becky.

"So what then is the matter? You look troubled," she said seriously.

"It's nothing really," I lied again once more.

"I can fix it. I promise, no matter what it is, all you have to do is tell me about what's bothering you," Becky said.

"I wish you could, but there is no way that you can fix it, unless you're a miracle worker," I said. I'm scared of darkness. I've not found myself in this kind of condition before in my entire life, and as for the mosquitoes, I know that they'll kill me before tomorrow morning."

"Oh, poor you," Becky replied calmly.

"Is that all that you can say, I thought you promised to fix it no matter what. Anyway, I knew that you'd be just as helpless about this," I told Becky with a mocking laugh.

"Says who?" she grinned.

"But it's the truth," I replied.

"Cheer up, Sandra, my father has made arrangements for a generator-set so that we'll have proper electricity," said Becky as we walked back to our room.

"Do you mean that there's going to be electricity later?" I asked excitedly.

"Yeah! And also there'll be a story-telling session tonight," Becky told me.

"A story telling-session, what's that supposed to mean?" I asked.

"Granddad is hosting a story session tonight as part of your welcoming ceremony," Becky answered.

"What? Haven't I already had the most marvellous reception today, this is becoming so embarrassing, I guess I'll just have to remain in the room while you guys will be out there celebrating," I said seriously.

"No, you can't do that to Grandma and Grandpa. They're both well respected in this community and, more to the point, story-telling means a lot to our people and they don't joke with it. At times like this, everybody assembles together to listen to the stories, and so will you tonight," she said honestly.

"I don't know, I'll have to think about that before they start," I said.

I heard my father was talking to the gong-master to summon all the villagers this evening," Becky said.

"Do you see why I'll like to stay indoors, Granddad will certainly talk about me and I'll be so embarrassed," I said grudgingly.

"If I were you I'll be so proud, Granddad used to think that he wouldn't live long enough to see the day that you'd come and see him and Grandma. He'd lost hope before, you know, since after all these years your Dad hasn't come back to visit them. That's the reason he is so thrilled about tonight's story session. You'll listen to some of his favourite stories," Becky explained.

"I suppose you're right, and I quite appreciate what he's doing, but I still don't see why he has to make so much fuss about this," I replied.

"You still don't understand, Sandra. You're the first white—pardon me—mulatto or whatever. Sandra, let me tell you the truth, your skin compared to everyone else's in this village, you're a *white girl*, mulatto or not. And like I said, Granddad is simply too happy to see you. To him, you are his little princess, and that's exactly how he wants to treat you, so be patient with him. It's not going to be every single day," Becky told me bluntly.

"Yeah right! Some princess that I am," I sighed.

"Please promise me that you won't let him down, you've got to come out and watch, and I give you my word you're going to enjoy yourself too," Becky said pleadingly.

"Okay, I'll come out, if it'll make him feel honoured and appreciated," I said.

True to Becky's words, the generator guys later came around and had it wired around the compound, and soon the compound was lit up. It became so bright. It attracted so many people, as well as fun-loving insects and flies as they gathered around the fluorescent lights outside.

"Thanks, Sandra," Becky replied happily.

"Do you mind telling me what Granddad was talking about *Jerusalem* during his welcome speech in the living room earlier?" I said to Becky.

"You don't want to know about that. Grandpa and all the lots in this village believe that the names of all the places in the Holy Bible such as Egypt, Israel, Jerusalem and the rest of them are all up in heaven and their hope is that one day when they die, they'll all go to these places," Becky said, to my amusement.

"You must be kidding, are you sure he really thinks that?" I said to Becky.

"Wish I was just kidding, but you see—the people in this community all think and believe different things, you know," Becky said.

"Take this for example: my grandma—I mean my mum's mother—refused to come and visit us in Lagos because she believes that our house must smell very awful, as the toilet is right in the house and not in a big flowing river like the one in the village. My mum had tried many times to convince her that we do flush the toilet after every use, and that our house doesn't smell, but she simply wasn't convinced and refused to have a change of mind," Becky said, amusingly.

"These are some of the funniest things that I've ever heard in my entire life," I said, laughing hysterically.

Later, Becky and I went back to our room to have some rest before the *show* (story telling) began in earnest.

CHAPTER THIRTEEN
Folk Tales

I had a funny feeling that Becky, herself, wasn't too sure about where Jerusalem was, in heaven or on earth. As we lay in bed trying to get a bit of peace and quiet time, or rather struggling with the hot sweat, which was caused by extreme heat inside the room, I attempted to find out the truth about Becky's knowledge about the topic really.

"Can I ask you a question, Becky?" I said.

"Sure, what about?" she enquired.

"Do you really know where Jerusalem is?" I asked openly.

"What silly questions, but hang on a minute—you're thinking that I'm just as dumb as the rest of them in this village, aren't you?" Becky said snappily.

"Sorry, there is no need for you to get so upset, I'm just curious," I said.

"Curious about what, that I don't know that Jerusalem is somewhere on earth rather than in heaven?" she retorted.

"All right, I'm sorry. Case closed, okay?" I said ruefully.

"There's one thing, though," said Becky uncertainly. "I find it a little unbelievable that Egypt is really an African country."

"Don't make me laugh, Becky, I thought we just ended that argument. Besides, I thought that you knew everything already. And what's so strange about Egypt being an African country anyway?" I asked.

"Don't know, can't explain why," she admitted.

"Very well then, I wonder what sort of things you learn in your school," I said. "Anyway, just in case you find yourself in a similar argument in future, I thought you should know that Egypt is really an African country, and not in a different continent, ok?"

"Thanks anyway! Pity my father also thinks like Granddad," she mumbled.

"How do you mean?" I asked her.

"Not just grandpa, but my father believes also that Egypt is in heaven," said Becky.

"What? This isn't happening, why should Uncle Bill—a former school head-teacher also think something like that? I mean if everyone else didn't know the truth about so many things in this area, at least as a former head-teacher he was supposed to enlighten them, not sink with them. In fact, he is supposed to represent all retired head-teachers in this community," I said, infuriated.

With my last reaction, Becky ran out of the room to call her dad to come and listen to what I just said about Egypt being in Africa.

"Papa come and hear this," she yelled loudly.

"What are you calling your dad for? If you make any fuss about this, you'll make a fuss about just anything," I said.

"What is happening over there? What's the matter?" Uncle Bill asked, as he came running.

"Don't panic, Uncle Bill. Everything's fine," I said sharply.

"Sandra just told me that Egypt is an African country," Becky said to her dad.

"In our very own Africa you mean?" asked Uncle Bill, disbelieving.

"I don't believe that you don't know this either, Uncle Bill," I said quietly.

"Um, you see, it's not that I didn't know before, but it's eh, like in the ch…"

"Is there anyone of you over there who would like to tell me where Egypt is?" Uncle Bill shouted unexpectedly to the crowd in the other room.

"In heaven!" they all chorused simultaneously.

"No way, people, we've all been so wrong. My niece here said that everybody elsewhere in the world except us in this village knows that Egypt, Israel, and all those countries, which we read about from the Bible, actually exist here on earth.

"And Egypt, in particular, is in this our continent— Africa," Uncle Bill announced to all those people, who'd been sitting there all day, enjoying their locally brewed gin.

"I'm not surprised this is coming from you, Mr. Bill, because I don't see you in church anymore, or possibly you've been drinking too much alcohol," said one fellow from the crowd.

"A little white girl with a little white lie! I'm not so surprised that this is coming from her," said another grubby-looking fellow from the crowd.

When Becky had explained to me all the confusion that was going on, I felt somehow annoyed and irritated, but thought that perhaps it wasn't entirely their fault.

They simply didn't know. I came out to talk to them later, and with the help of Uncle Bill was able to convince them that those places do actually exist in this very earth.

However, expectedly, before the start of the story session, Granddad gave another long speech, only this time he announced that he was going to confer me with a new name in the local dialect, as I didn't already have one. The crowd cheered with clapping and urged Granddad to go on, that I so deserved it.

"Come here, my daughter," he said, directing me to sit on a wooden chair next to my grandma. Then Uncle Bill's wife came out very quickly with a shiny, multi-coloured, beaded piece of cloth and spread it around the chair before I sat down.

"No matter where you go, you'll always remember to come back here. This is your root, and from today onward, you will be known and called 'Izibeya,' (There is God)," grandpa said, as he poured some gin to the ground.

A loud applause followed immediately after he completed his statement. Then my dad's youngest brother, Uncle Loco, broke two coconuts and used the coconut water to wash my hands and feet after some more rituals were performed.

The village Chief, who was also present, offered prayers for me, and then opened the session with his first story. A lot more people took their turns afterwards as the stories were told, so plenty of folk songs were sung and the drummers happily beat to the tunes as the people clapped and danced.

I must admit that I hadn't seen anything like it before, an entire village—children and adults gathering together just to listen to folk tales. And it turned out to be the most hilarious night for me. They might not have such things like the television to keep them entertained, but they sure do have their own unique way of entertaining themselves.

The best of the stories interpreted to me was one told by Grandpa, himself, about the cunning witch doctor. Two barren women needed spiritual help from a certain witch doctor so they could become pregnant. The witch doctor had told the two women that he can help them, but they should be prepared to make some sacrifices. He said to them openly that they would go mad after the birth of their first babies. One of the women said that she wasn't ready to go bananas just because she wanted to have a child, while the second woman said that she was prepared to do whatever there was to do, which could help her to become pregnant and eventually give birth to her own child. She agreed with the witch doctor and asked him to go ahead to do what he thought would be helpful to her, in order to have a baby. When the were about to leave the witch-doctor's house, he gave some kind of charm to the one who was prepared, and he also told her what to do with it when she got back to her house.

Soon after that visit to the witch doctor, the woman became pregnant and nine months later her first baby was born. The following year, she gave birth to a second baby, and by then the woman was feeling very apprehensive that the time for her to pay her ultimate prize was near and might not be able to care for her kids by herself for too long, so she made special arrangements with a trusted family member to take care of her kids should something terrible happened to her. That didn't happen, however. Instead, in the year that followed, she became pregnant one more time and later gave birth to a pair of twins.

She'd been ready to pay the ultimate price, but surprisingly she didn't go crazy at all.

Meanwhile, the other lady who'd been watching to see when the woman would go mad became so disappointed and frustrated that she changed her mind and went back to the witch doctor to inform him that she was now prepared to go through with whatever that he was going to do as she'd been watching to see the other woman go crazy, but she did not, even after giving birth to four healthy babies.

The witch doctor only laughed, and then told the lady that he only used the word 'mad' as a phrase to describe mothers, because he believed that after a woman gives birth to her first baby and the baby starts to grow, the mother automatically becomes *crazy*, you know but not crazy as in real *madness* though, but you see that from then on all she tends to do is work, work and worry until she becomes stressed up completely. And to him that is being *socially mad*. However, the witch doctor told the woman disappointedly that it was too late for him to do anything to help her, as he'd just retired from his work a few days earlier.

However, listening to grandpa's lovely story had brought my mind back to what I said earlier about speaking in parables. The witch doctor clearly spoke to the two women in parable, and one of them was fooled by his words, I felt sorry for the poor woman, anyone who love life could easily fall into the same kind of trap. But thanks goodness it was only a fairy-tale.

CHAPTER FOURTEEN
Circumcision

We were so, so tired by the time the story session was over; everyone went back to their houses so late in the night. Having slept very late in the night, we were in bed, snoring like two over-fed pigs, even though it had been morning since until Uncle Loco's 9-year-old son, Victor, came to knock on the door, thereby disturbing our precious morning siesta.

It was the last day in his school and he wanted Becky and me to come and watch the closing ceremony as observed at the end of every school term. Usually, the headmaster would announce the names of pupils who had worked very hard to pass their exams and move to the next class at the commencement in the following school year. Generally, the first two terms of school is usually not a big deal, but the going gets very tough, because if you fail to pass your exams in the last term of the year and your name is not called out by the head teacher, then it means that you're not among the hardworking pupils and will therefore repeat the same old class in the next school year. In that instance, many tears would flow from those who can't make it to the next class.

Becky later told me that such days were always with mixed emotions for the school children and parents alike. Those who've worked hard enough and have passed their exams would be very happy together with their parents and guardians, while the opposite emotion is what runs through those who have failed to work hard.

I promised little Victor that we'd be there to show our support no matter what.

The early morning sun shone brightly and beautifully and I didn't want to stay in bed any longer. I wanted to go out and just walk around and take, as much sun as I possibly could, and also get a feel of the fresh, gentle wind that was blowing around freely, which of course your eyes can't really see, except for the tall grasses swaying from side to side.

Soon there was another knock on the door, and this time it was Tessie's mum. She brought in two buckets of water for Becky and I to bath with. Becky rose up from her bed and took the buckets of water from her step-mum and dropped the two buckets in the bathroom. When she came out from the bathroom, she went and stood beside the window. She raised the curtains and looked out.

She'd been looking outside for more than ten minutes and I thought most probably that she was simply enjoying the warm rays coming from the sun. She didn't seem to want to stop looking outside. I began to be nosy just to find out why she was glued to the window.

"Are you ever going to get tired of standing there?" I asked.

"I don't know. I feel so sorry for her whenever I see her," she said whisperingly.

"Who do you feel sorry for this early morning? I thought you were stuck there because of the beautiful sun outside," I said.

"Just come and take a look. Its not that I like staring at other people, but I can't help to stare anytime I see her," she repeated.

"Who do you want me to look at?" I asked as I walked towards the window.

"Isn't she beautiful?" asked Becky. "She look so pretty and calm, and yet so useless. I don't understand why terrible things keep happening to innocent children."

"Are you referring to her, and why do you say that she's useless? I mean, what's wrong with her?" I asked so impatiently, staring outside at this young, beautiful girl. She was sitting down on a mat and staring into the empty space in front of her as if she was in static shock.

"You don't want to know what happened to her. It's a long story," Becky responded with a sad expression on her face.

"I want to know. Did she go mad or something?" I asked, worried.

"I remember when my parents were still married and all of us lived in this village. Then, this house wasn't built yet. What I'm trying to say is that the space where this house is now standing used to be empty at the time apart from some remaining patches of walls from grandpa's old house, and a lot of children used to gather to play together most of the times. And you know what? Her and me were like best friends back then. We did a lot of things together, you know, such things like running around playing hide and seek, or sometimes chasing after butterflies flying in the air and lizards. Something very funny happened one day when she came with her baby brother who was only learning to crawl. Ruth had left him on his own as we were busy running about, and the baby started to cry, he had grabbed a small millipede, Becky continued with a small smile dancing on her lips. You know, the one that has lots and lots of legs, which must have crawling from the ground and bit it. By the time we got to him his mouth had turned blood red and it remained like that for nearly two weeks. It was so gross. It used to be so much fun back then. And now she hardly remembers anything," Becky explained unhappily.

"I still don't get you. What exactly happened to her?" I asked curiously.

"She was only ten years old when her parents had her circumcised. You know what that is, don't you? Becky turned to ask me. 'Female-Genital-Mutilation.' That's what most people prefer to call it. And in case you don't fully understand what it means, I suggest you check it up in your dictionary, or ask your teacher to explain it to you when you get back to your school in Ireland," Becky said, looking quite disturbed.

"Is it something that serious?" I asked innocently.

"Yes, it is. Actually it is very dangerous, and it keeps happening to nearly all the girls in this community, and it's so sad that nobody ever does anything to stop it from happening to more and more girls," she replied.

"I must have heard about it before, but I didn't know that it was something really terrible," I said.

"See that girl? Her name is Ruth and she is one of the most unlucky girls because the day that she was circumcised, the voodoo priestess who performed the operation had operated wrongly on her because she was so drunk. And with too many mistakes, the poor girl had to go through that horrible experience all over again the next day," Becky said, and went on to explain the procedures to me.

"What? That's gross," I said.

"Ruth couldn't bear the terrible pains and she simply passed out."

"But, unfortunately for her, when she did come 'round, she couldn't remember anything whatsoever. Not who she was, nor her parents and she didn't even remember the excessive pain, that caused her to pass out in the first place. And she's been like that ever since," Becky explained to me, nearly gnashing her teeth.

"That's a horrible thing to happen to any child. But why do some parents allow their own children to undergo such unnecessary agony?" I asked Becky with the most repulsive feelings.

"Don't know, I can't say why," she answered. "I was about seven years of age when my parents arranged the same thing for me, I was completely terrified, and went and hid myself under a big mango tree behind the school building, I hung about there until I got bitten by a slimy green snake. And so..."

"I don't believe Uncle Bill would want to do something like that to you. Did he not know the risks involved?" I asked Becky.

"I beg your pardon? My dad lives in this village and, therefore, must partake in the things that take place here, right or wrong," Becky answered.

But that type of behaviour is not nice, people shouldn't do something just because everyone else does. I'm sure that if it were the kids behaving in such a pitiful manner, the adults would be quick to tag it as 'peer pressure,' I thought to myself.

"You must have been scared when the snake bit you. How did you find help?" I asked Becky.

"I forgot to mention to you that my maternal grandmother is an herbalist, and she'd showed me some leaves before and talked about the effectiveness of each one of them. Luckily for me, I looked around and recognised one of such leaves, which has a powerful antidote to snake poison. So I crawled next to it and cut one leaf off, and then squeezed the juice on the wound."

"I later walked out to the school compound with the aid of a walking stick, and then someone saw me and helped me home. My dad was very upset with me; he said that I didn't have to go into hiding just because of F.G.M., that it was customary after all, and that I couldn't run away from it really; however, I was excused from that first attempt because of the snake bite. But I couldn't keep running away like my dad told me—the second time they got me and I was cut," said Becky bluntly.

"Cut? Just like that, was it really painful?" I asked shockingly.

"Stupid question, Sandra. What do feel if you mistakenly cut yourself with a razor blade?" she asked, upset, a bitter expression on her face. "You know the answer obviously, don't you?"

"I'm sorry, Becky. I'm just so shocked, that's all," I said.

"Don't apologise, you weren't there and, besides, if you lived here, you would have had to go through the same thing as well. I said that was the most painful, sickening, and disgusting thing I've ever had to go through in my entire life. Sorry, *second most disgusting thing that happened to me*," Becky added sadly.

"I feel utterly gutted just listening to these odd stories, especially when the children don't have a choice," I said angrily.

"Well, I was lucky not to have ended up like her. I mean like Ruth," Becky said finally, and then she walked away from the small window.

After we'd eaten the breakfast, which Tessie's mum had prepared for us that morning, Becky and I headed towards the direction of the school, which was about a twenty minute walk.

Other parents and relatives of pupils surrounded everywhere inside the large school compound and peered into what seemed like the assembly hall. We could hear the children making so much noise inside the hall. I looked beside me and saw one lady praying eagerly. Becky whispered to me in a mocking tone of voice that I shouldn't pay much attention to the lady.

Her reasons being that many women in the village forgot to bear in mind the importance of encouraging their children to do their homework when they came back from school, instead of "oh you're back from school, drop your school bag and lets head to the farm immediately" But she's now fearful that her son might not make it to the next class. That is what most of them do, Becky said accusingly. Of course they need their children to help out with farm work too but, the difference is, they should learn to do first thing first."

"Why do you think they do that?" I asked sharply.

"She wouldn't bother to pray if her chid was a girl, because in this community, people still believed that the education of the 'girl child' less important. They're more interested to send their daughters into early marriage as soon as they turn fourteen or fifteen, and in some cases thirteen," Becky explained to me.

"Oh, not again!" I exclaimed. "But why do all the stories around here have to be so sad and uncivilized. I personally can't imagine myself already married at this age, I said. That is so disgusting."

Soon the bellboy came out of the door, and started to ring the school bell, which brought an immediate silence in the hall, and all the parents and guardians began to move closer and closer to the nearest view of them. Then I looked straight to the other end and saw a boy staring lustfully at Becky.

"It looks like someone's got a secret admirer," I said playfully.

"Who's is it?" Becky asked me, hoping that I wasn't referring to her.

"Look at that boy over there, he's been looking at you for ages, I wonder why you haven't noticed him yet," I said, pointing at him.

"Don't mind that good for nothing idiot. He's a loser," Becky simpered.

"So you noticed him. Maybe you should introduce us," I said teasingly.

"Why? There's nothing between that vain boy and me," she responded.

"It doesn't seem like that to me. Perhaps you're only pretending," I said.

Becky glanced quickly at the boy once more and he smiled openly at her, as though the two were best mates. Just then, we were interrupted by the headmaster's announcement. He spoke in simple and correct English just like Uncle Bill.

The headmaster started to call out the names of the lucky pupils, class after class. When it got to Victor's class, I noticed that my heart had suddenly started to beat faster than usual. Thankfully in the end, Victor's name was called amongst the pupils who had worked hard to pass their exams, and was due to go to the next class the coming session. Interestingly, he came in fifth place and I felt very proud of him.

Uncle Loco invited Becky and me for dinner at his place that evening to mark Victor's impressive exam results. Uncle Loco's house was a pleasant-looking, small bungalow. It had three bedrooms, and he lived there with his wife, Julia, Victor and his baby sister, Molly. Julia served a delicious meal of fresh fish pepper soup and boiled yam. After we had finished eating the food, Julia asked us to baby-sit for her while she rushed to buy some cold soft drinks from a small shop nearby. That caused me to wonder how they managed to have cold drinks without having electricity supply in the village.

Nonetheless, Julia explained to me later when I asked her, that the store owners usually bought blocks of ice from the big town nearby, and cleverly use it to keep the drinks cool in a big container and sold it from there.

We had a wonderful evening at uncle Loco's, and on our way back to, should I say my dad's house, we met a friend of Becky's who informed us about a forthcoming wedding the next day.

"Hello!" the girl said to Becky and me.

"Hello!" we both chorused at the same time.

"How come you didn't come to my place, when you heard that I was back from Lagos?" asked Becky.

"I'm really sorry, the girl said, awkwardly. I was going to, but I've been busy helping out with Philo's wedding arrangements."

"Do you mean to tell me that Philo is getting married, and to whom anyway?" Becky asked, shocked.

"I think you know Monica's father? She is going to marry him tomorrow as his..."

"As his what? Excuse me, but Monica's father has two wives already," Becky said, interrupting.

"Yeah, she's going to become his third wife," the girl replied.

"This is so not good. Philo has sold her childhood to that old man,

and not only that, she definitely is going to become a slave to those two older women," Becky said angrily.

"Anyway, I hope you're not still angry with me for not turning up at your place, and I hope you'll bring your 'white' cousin to the wedding tomorrow," she said to Becky.

"No. I'm not angry at you, but I'm not so sure about tomorrow," Becky replied to the girl.

"Don't mind her, we shall be there tomorrow," I cut in.

"Yeah sure, we'll see you around tomorrow. Bye," Becky said slowly as we turned to walk away also.

"Tell me about this wedding," I said to Becky, demandingly.

"Isn't this typical of what I was talking to you about earlier in the school compound? You won't believe me if I told you her age. I mean, Philo, she's only thirteen, agreed she's very tall, but she's still only a child," Becky said, wheezing.

"You don't mean that, what about her education?" I asked, confusedly.

"Yeah right! You're talking about education when the greatest aspiration for most of the girls in this community is to get married and have children, that's all, because it is how their mind was programmed from an early age," Becky explained.

That was more shocking for me to hear, and just imagine any sensible parents could openly allow their young daughter to get married to an older man who is already married with two or more wives and have many children? I know that Becky later told me that poverty was partly responsible for many of them. She also said that, by giving their daughters' hands in marriage so early, the parents hope to receive extra financial help from their in-laws.

You can only imagine how sickening that sounded to me, and I wondered how early I would have been forced into joining or becoming a part of the *early marriage syndrome* if my dad hadn't had the opportunity to have travelled to Europe and settled down there. However, I can only be thankful to my own star that I wasn't born there. I think that it is only too obvious that these young girls are victims of all these unusual practices. Pity neither me nor Becky could do anything to change the situation.

CHAPTER FIFTEEN
Wedding Day

I thought very carefully the next morning about attending the so-called wedding. First of all I didn't know the soon-to-be-bride, Philo, and so I couldn't find any good reason to attend, after all I hadn't been present at any such wedding that had anything to do with an under-aged bride before.

"I'm not so sure about attending the wedding," I told Becky.

"Blimey! Yesterday, you tried to disregard my doubts about attending this wedding. I'm surprised it's your turn today. Whatever happens we've got to be there, if only for you to witness how marriages are done in our area," Becky said.

I helped Uncle Bill's wife later to feed the chickens with some dried corns while Becky cleaned around the house. After we'd eaten, Grandma and Grandpa summoned us to the sitting room for a chat. They asked me all sorts of questions about Ireland, my friends and my school, but mostly about my mum. Afterwards, I was able to share some photographs that I'd brought with me from Ireland with them. I guess Becky got a little tired of interpreting as she soon complained of headaches.

Back at our room later, Becky and I talked about the usual girly bits and pieces; you know, stuff like fashion, school and the boys, but I was really careful not to raise any topic that would make her feel irritated and spoil our, if she suddenly remembered any of the ugly things that happened to her.

All the same, we still had really nice times just talking together like really close pals.

When it was time for us to go out to the wedding venue, I was lost to find something suitable, but Becky insisted that I was okay even with the same clothes that I'd had on since in the morning.

"You still look glamorous even in those, why don't you stop making so much fuss about what's best and what's not to wear to the wedding. I'm sure you'll still win the best-dressed girl if there was a competition at the wedding venue," she said convincingly.

Finally, I decided to wear my new pair of cropped brown trousers, cream colour sleeveless shirt and my new black high-heeled boots. I brushed my hair to the back and tied it in a single knot, and was quite impressed at seeing myself in the mirror. I imagined that Becky might not have something to match what I was wearing, and so I persuaded her to wear one of mine (a sleeveless knee length flowery chiffon gown).

Her hair was braided in dread-locks and it matched very well with the outfit.

Soon we started to hear the sound of loud music coming from the direction of the *Town Hall*, which was the wedding venue.

As we arrived at the venue, people turned to look at us. I guess they hadn't before seen a girl my age so dressed up like I was, especially with my long hair. They must have thought that my dressing especially was out of this world, you know, coupled with the *white girl* stuff. I almost felt guilty as all the other girls looked at me with envy. It was clear that their type of fashion could not match with the simplest of my clothing.

"So where's the bride?" I asked Becky, as I sneaked a quick look through the crowds of people, all sitting expectantly.

We took our seats in a corner where Becky was sure we'd get a good view of the happenings.

"I'm sure, she'll be coming out any minute now," Becky replied excitedly.

In not so long, a dark tall man took the microphone and began to make announcements. I assumed he was the master of ceremony (MC).

"He's here again," Becky whispered, pointing at a group of boys who were standing on the other side of the venue.

"Who is it?" I asked.

"Don't you remember him, that same boy we saw at the school compound yesterday —Michael," she said.

"Oh, your boyfriend! I didn't know that he was called Michael," I replied, jokingly.

"Quit referring to him as my boyfriend. He is not, and will never be, okay?" Becky said snappily.

"Why are you pretending to hate him so much? It seems like you fancy him, and I think that something is definitely going on between you two," I said, suspiciously.

"No way! I don't like him and I'm definitely not going to marry him, or any other boy from this village for that matter," Becky said.

"Wait-a-minute! Am I missing something here?" I queried.

"Not so, please," Becky replied swiftly.

"Don't tell me that that boy asked you to marry him, or is there some other secret that you're keeping from me?" I asked.

"I knew you wont understand."

"You knew I wont understand what? I queried anxiously. You can tell me anything, remember?"

"I hate to tell you this, but the answers to your question earlier is yes. Don't get me wrong, it's not like he asked me directly to marry him," she said. "But it's just one of those things."

"What are you talking about?" I asked, confused.

"There's something else about that boy and me that I haven't told you," Becky said shyly.

"I knew there was something, I said as though it was a matter of life and death. So are you going to tell me what it is or not?"

We'd been so engrossed in the argument that we almost forgot the reason we were there. Later, she told me the reason why she disliked Michael so much, not like anything was his fault.

"It's a long story, she said, and then continued. And it all began as a game in the village, a type of dating game, you know, The boys in the village started it a long time ago, it's not like you have to go on a date with anyone. Each year they'd write a list containing the names of all teenage boys and girls who in only in their imaginations obviously, were likely to get married to each other in the future. On the lists, they sort of matched each boy's name to that of any girl, and have the lists plastered at conspicuous places around the whole village."

It happened that Becky's name was paired to that of Michael's, surprisingly Michael had taken it very seriously, and so had other members of his family, who thought that Becky is going to make the perfect wife for their son. And they have been calling her *daughter-in-law* since then. Now that is definitely the most bizarre type of match making game that I've ever heard about, no wonder Becky seemed so embarrassed to talk about it.

It sounded like a serious matter, but I couldn't help but laugh. *I've definitely watched a variety of dating game shows on television before, but haven't seen or heard of anything like this one. This surely is one hell of a journey that I'm not going to forget in a hurry. Ever since I arrived, it's been from one funny or weird story to the other.*

"What's your problem?" Becky bawled suddenly.

I didn't know that Michael had also sighted us from where he was standing with the other boys and had moved over to over to our side. I turned around and saw that Michael of a boy smiling sheepishly at Becky. I was getting a bit worried too because I thought he could be stalking Becky. I didn't know why he always seemed to pop up wherever we were.

"Why don't you just ignore him, there's no need for you to be resentful towards him. I'm sure it wasn't his fault that your name was paired with his," I said.

"Yeah, but I just want him to know that no matter what he might be dreaming up in that ugly head of his is nothing but delusion and he should, therefore, keep his distance from me. And I don't know why you are being protective of him, you don't even know what he's like," Becky said crossly.

"Don't say that, I'm not been protective of him. I guess I'm just curious," I replied calmly.

"What exactly are you being curious about anyway, can't you see that I'm being followed?" Becky asked.

"I'm curious about what will happen if, I mean, just like the other girls around here, Uncle Bill decides to make you abandon your education and marry someone at this age," I said.

"I apologise, Sandra. I should have known that you were only concerned about me. Perhaps I should let you know that I'm a bit sceptical too as to whether my father is having some secret marriage plans on my behalf with Michael's family," Becky said.

"What makes you think that he'll do something like that against your wish?" I asked.

"Simple," she replied. "Because that is what goes on around here. It's in our tradition that parents of both the boy and the girl pre-arrange their children's' marriage, and you just don't have a choice."

"This is outrageously insane," I snapped. "You mean you don't have a choice to choose who you fall in love with?"

"Fall in love, indeed! Now that is another ball game entirely, in this community you don't need to or to a certain extent, you don't really have the right to fall in love with anyone, Becky said. And mark you, that word 'love' is almost not allowed and nearly perceived by the elders as a taboo in this area. Young children especially are most probably not supposed to discuss love openly."

On hearing this, I burst out laughing; imagine a boy and a girl getting married without being in-love, Becky said that they didn't need to, but once they're a couple, they learn to live in love, and gradually they fall in love with each other in due course. However Becky seemed a little upset because I laughed, it didn't go quite well with her, she seriously thought I was making fun of the situation, but I wasn't and that is truth. I mean, how can I bare to make fun of something that serious, besides, when I know how much it affects her.

"What's so funny about what I said? I can see that all this amuses you," she replied angrily. "Isn't it because you're so lucky to have been born in a wiser world?"

"Hey! Don't think that I'm making fun of you because I laughed, I just feel sad for all you lot around here," I said apologetically.

"I'm sorry, I didn't mean to take to take it out on you. Anyway, it's no use and it's not your fault either," she said, regrettably.

"Why don't we forget about all that for now, we need to concentrate so that I'll catch the bride's face clearly with my camera when she pops out. I said, persuasively. Do you think that there is a better position?"

"Don't worry, this is the best position," Becky said happily.

Soon the music started to play very, very loud. They'd hired a generator and had the sound systems connected to it. The town hall was fully lit with fluorescent lights as well and everywhere looked bright and fit for a proper wedding venue.

Later a group of women dressed uniformly turned out to dance to the music and everyone cheered at them. I wondered which among them was the bride, but Becky said that none of them were, as the women were merely entertainers. Nonetheless, we did not wait too long before another group came out. This time they came out in two long lines; young beautiful maidens each covered from their head to toe with very pretty cotton prints.

We watched excitedly while Becky explained the reasons behind those veils, she said that their heads were covered deliberately in a bid to confuse the groom because he was expected to carefully pick from among the maidens, which one was his bride and unveil her only, as any mistake of unveiling the wrong girl would lead to a big fine. And in order to prevent that from happening, most couples chose to cheat their way out, to avoid paying a fine.

Becky said that all they have to is come to some kind of agreement, whereby the bride allows the groom to see the type of shoes that she was going to wear well in advance, and in that case, all that he— the groom need to do was concentrate on the ground and check out the shoes on the legs on each of the maidens.

"Wow! Now this is interesting, sounds like some kind of game," I wondered aloud as I positioned my camera, set to capture the most important moment of the day.

Then the MC began to talk again, interrupting the music. He spoke clearly in English. That was because generally, when there was an important event-taking place in the village, a lot of people from neighbouring clans who spoke a different dialect also liked to attend so as a courtesy, they usually spoke in English.

"This is show time," the MC announced at the full volume of the microphone. "The groom will now have to prove to everyone in this hall today that no matter whether he is blindfolded, he can tell who his beautiful bride is."

"Watch! Here comes the groom," Becky said hurriedly, pointing to three middle-aged men and two women heavily dressed in native attire walking towards the maidens.

"But which one of them?" I asked Becky disappointedly, as none of the men looked young enough to be the groom to a supposedly 13-year-old girl.

"That one, the one in the middle with the goatee beards," she replied breathlessly.

"I don't get it, Becky, that's an old man. I don't mean old as in *old*, but he's nothing like anyone that'll be marrying a girl of thirteen years. That is so disgusting," I added.

"C'mon, Sandra! Set your camera, we're here to have fun, remember?" said Becky carelessly.

I reluctantly took a photo of him as he walked around the girls, looking at each one of them very closely. Then, he suddenly stopped in his tracks as he got nearer to a certain maiden. He walked around her, looking at her from top to bottom. And finally, he unveiled her and everyone cheered and applauded, as well as Becky and I.

"She's so beautiful, isn't she?" said Becky cheerfully.

I watched, spellbound, unable to put together what I was looking at, she looked so pretty, pure and innocent. But looking at the man she was marrying was despicable. I hadn't imagined that the bride would be so pretty, and sweet like an angel.

"No," I thought out loud.

"Sorry?" queried Becky.

"I mean, yeah, she's beautiful—and young—and, in fact, I can't believe that she is the bride to that man," I said, and regrettably put my camera back inside my handbag.

"What are you talking about?" Becky asked.

"I can't stay to watch this, I don't mean to sound like this, but this is unthinkable. Is she an orphan or something? That man is old enough to be her grandfather," I retorted.

"I know, but let's not bother ourselves about that now, we're only here to watch and have fun, you know," said Becky. "And to answer your question, she's not an orphan."

"Look over there, that's her father, and if he's not bothered, then why should we be the ones to bother."

You see those two women sitting side by side with the groom, those are his first and second wives, and they have nine children altogether. Philo is going to be his third wife," Becky said to me.

"Enough, I think that you should stop telling me about it. I feel disgusted already," I said, frustrated.

I'd been so shocked and baffled the moment the veil was taken off Philo's face. She sure didn't look very happy in her typical African attire, either. She seemed to me more like a rag doll dressed in an oversized frock than a happy bride. I thought that her parents must have pressured her into marrying that man so they could earn a bride price. Instead of being happy, I felt sorry for her because I felt that maybe if she really had a choice, she wouldn't give up her future for that stupid marriage.

CHAPTER SIXTEEN
Poems

When we got back to the house at the end of the wedding ceremony, I was very upset still and refused to reply Uncle Bill's warm greetings. I ignored him to avoid a sudden outburst of rudeness as a result of the anger that I felt in me.

I soon remembered what my mum used to tell me back in Ireland, that whenever I felt really upset, I should write down exactly those things that had caused me to be hurting in the first place. And that worked well for me all the time, because usually, by the time I'd finish writing down all the stuff that made me to be sad, I always found that the pain had disappeared. But in that annoyance, I decide to do some painting instead. I told Becky what I intended to do, though she acted as if she knew nothing about painting.

"What! You mean painting the bedroom walls?" Becky asked annoyingly.

"Not very funny, Becky, and don't tell me that you didn't do sketches or drawings in your school," I said.

"I was only joking around," she replied, laughing.

"Good, because that's the type of painting that I'm talking about," I replied her.

"In that case, you'll need a blackboard, and some chalks, and, wait a minute, do you have any of these things?" she asked, concerned.

"Not to worry, I have all my stuff in my bag," I said, as I pulled out my drawing pad and pencils and began to arrange them on the only table in the room.

'I'm going to paint everything that I saw at the wedding, especially the husband. I'll make sure he looks like a frightful monster in my paintings by the time I finish with it," I said firmly.

"What's come over you? Don't tell me that you're still annoyed,"

"Of course I am still annoyed," I replied angrily.

"Soothe yourself," Becky replied coolly.

"Whatever," I said, and continued to spread out the writing pad and other stuff on the only table.

"I've got a better idea about what we should do; I suggest we write poems for each other. You'll keep mine and I'll keep yours and, with that, we'll always remember each other after you've gone back to Ireland," Becky said.

"Brilliant idea, why didn't you say this to me earlier? But hang on a minute, what type of poems should we write about," I asked.

"Why don't you write a poem about Ireland, and I'll write one about Nigeria," she said, as we soon got down to writing.

Becky's Poem, *Africa, my Homeland*

The weather is so hot you want to go out for a swim.
You'd do that quite a lot and you could end up very trim.
A fiery sphere of flame is what we look up to each day
It could leave you hot and bothered when on the
    road in a delay.
The schools are very strict and in exams, if you don't
    pass...

You'll bear a great disgrace; you'll have to remain in
    the same class!
The clothes are quite exquisite and you can't
    describe their beauty
They're different designs for each tribe, from dark to
    bright and fruity.
The telly is such a bore but kids have better things to do.
Like story telling and wrestling...
Forget about your blues!
The music is quite awkward and I do admit
The dialogue is funny; it does leave us in a fit!
The foods are a variety of different tasty things
Although they're strange, they make a change from
    bread and chicken wings!

"Wow! This is a lovely poem Becky; I'll cherish it for the
rest of my life. It is definitely going to be the best reminder of
you," I said, after she read it to me.

"Thanks, I'm so happy that you like it," she replied.

My Poem, *Crescendo!*

Down, down it goes
Straight from heaven itself
Water crystals, soft white crescendo that shines as
    it comes down like little angels, with a message to tell
Filling our meadows, a white blanket
    sea of snow firm and rises every hour
    going gently down, no one hears any sound
    only feels the cold.
Most birds at home, only the brave
Ones that smile at the snow, then rustle their
    feathers.
Children come out to play, all kitted out
    to make snow angels.

Alas! Pure white rug turns a murky brown
But no matter, snow will fall and make it new again
The air feels nippy with frost in every corner
Oh! Star –shaded snowflakes fall on
Our tongues soft for a moment,
Then melt instantly, all tingly and nice
Cold hearts soften and warm for a moment
Snow reminds of a memory years ago
Let it fill beggars on the street with cascading peace
Families at home beside the fireplace telling
    stories and being cosy
Outside, feet deep in snow
An anklet only comfier

"What a brilliant poem you wrote," Becky said happily. "This is the best souvenir that we've got from each other."

"C'mon, let's go to the kitchen. I'm sure that Tessie's mum has prepared something delicious for us to eat."

CHAPTER SEVENTEEN
It's Only a Dream!

As I hurried to change into something more comfy, I heard the doorbell chime and I rushed to answer it.

"Sandra, sweetheart, you've got to wake up right now. It's been morning since, and your dad is already at the breakfast table waiting for you to come and join him."

"Mum!" I screamed out so loudly. I d–don't get it," I stammered, as I opened my eyes and saw my mum standing right next to my bed.

"What were you thinking? It isn't the weekend yet. You have to get up now and prepare for school quickly before you're late," Mum said, smiling.

"Good morning, Mum, I'll hurry up and get dressed right away," I said to Mum before she walked out of my room.

What a night! I don't believe that I've only been dreaming all this while. I hadn't really travelled to Africa in the first place, and yet I'd spent this marvellous time in just one night, I thought, while taking a quick shower in the bathroom.

Everything happened only in my dream. And, come to think of it, all those stories about Becky, Uncle Bill, Grandpa, poor Ruth, Philo and the rest of them, they'd only existed in my dream. And I reckon it was one bittersweet dream. However, I'll always remember that it is very important for people to be kind and thoughtful to those who have been through a rough time, regardless of who they are, their colour of skin or where they come from.

"Good morning, sweetheart, guess what? My dad told me as I sat down to eat my breakfast. We're going to Africa for two weeks,"

Wow, I wish everyone's dreams came true like this one. What do you think?

To be continued…

Final Note

The author has pledged a portion from the proceeds of this book to international development charity, Christian Aid, to support their good work in helping to expose the scandal of poverty, not only in Africa but the world over.

You can contact Christian Aid at 30 Wellington Park Belfast Bt9 6D, Northern Ireland. Tel: 028 903 81 204, or 17 Clanwilliam Terrace, Dublin 2, Ireland. Tel: +353 1 611 0801. Alternatively, you can visit their website www.christianaid.ie.

Printed in the United Kingdom
by Lightning Source UK Ltd.
106834UKS00001B/314